Enjoy all of these American Girl Mysteries:

THE SILENT STRANGER
A *Kaya* Mystery

PERIL AT KING'S CREEK
A *Felicity* Mystery

SECRETS IN THE HILLS
A *Josefina* Mystery

THE CURSE OF RAVENSCOURT
A *Samantha* Mystery

THE STOLEN SAPPHIRE
A *Samantha* Mystery

DANGER AT THE ZOO
A *Kit* Mystery

A SPY ON THE HOME FRONT
A *Molly* Mystery

— A *Josefina* MYSTERY —

SECRETS IN
THE HILLS

by Kathleen Ernst

★ American Girl™

Questions or comments? Call 1-800-845-0005, visit our Web site
at **americangirl.com**, or write Customer Service, American Girl,
8400 Fairway Place, Middleton, WI 53562-0497.

Printed in China
06 07 08 09 10 11 LEO 12 11 10 9 8 7 6 5 4 3

PICTURE CREDITS
The following individuals and organizations have generously
given permission to reprint illustrations contained in "Looking Back":
pp. 172–173—landscape, Jack Parsons Photography; portrait, Kit Carson
Home and Museum, Taos, NM; pp. 174–175—landscape, Jack Parsons
Photography; conquistador, University of Texas at El Paso, Texas Western
Press; map, Collections, Catholic Archdiocese of Santa Fe; pp. 176–177—
silver chalice, Mexico late 18th century, Alejandro Canas (born 1755).
Museum of International Folk Art, Santa Fe, NM, Dept. of Cultural Affairs.
Cat. No. FA 1989.28-1. Photo by Paul Smutko; illustration of Pueblo Revolt,
The Denver Public Library, Western History Collection; Comanche girls,
National Anthropological Archives, National Museum of Natural History/
Smithsonian Institution; pp. 178–179—cautiva (Refugio Gurriola), Kit Carson
Home and Museum, Taos, NM; Santa Fe Trail, North Wind Picture Archives;
unloading wagons, courtesy of the Richard F. Brush Art Gallery, St. Lawrence
University, Canton, NY; portraits of Josefa Jaramillo and Kit Carson,
Kit Carson Home and Museum, Taos, NM.

Illustrations by Jean-Paul Tibbles

Cataloging-in-Publication Data
available from the Library of Congress.

For Marsha—
forever in our hearts

Special thanks to
Sandra Jaramillo, Felipe Mirabal,
and the staff and volunteers of El Rancho
de las Golondrinas Living Museum
for their insights and support

TABLE OF CONTENTS

1
A SECRET SIGN

Josefina Montoya crouched in the autumn sun beside a prickly pear cactus. "Young prickly pear leaves can be used to help people with rheumatism," she recited. "Roasted older leaves can help children who have the mumps."

"Anything else?" Tía Magdalena prompted.

Josefina stared at the thick cactus pads, searching her memory.

"The juice is good for treating spider bites," Tía Magdalena reminded her.

After carefully using a small knife to scrape the leaves clean of their sharp spines and tiny, needle-like barbs, Josefina slid them into her collecting bag. "It's difficult to handle cactus without getting scratched," she said. "Almost as difficult as remembering all the cures you are teaching me! If I had a blank book, I'd write everything down."

Tía Magdalena smiled but shook her head. "A *curandera* doesn't need books," she told Josefina. "God provides true healers with everything they need—a good memory, a patient and loving heart, and two strong hands."

Josefina stared at her hands. Would they ever be as strong and knowing as Tía Magdalena's? Josefina believed she was meant to be a curandera, but sometimes she wondered if she would ever be able to remember half of what Tía Magdalena knew about healing.

Tía Magdalena seemed to know what Josefina was thinking. "It takes time," she said. "And you've already learned many things. There are wise women in the village, but I know you'll also be able to contribute if someone asks for help while I'm in Santa Fe."

"I'll do my best." Josefina felt a flutter of unease. Tía Magdalena rarely traveled, but she was leaving in the morning for a week's visit with Josefina's grandparents, Abuelito and Abuelita.

"All will be well." Tía Magdalena patted Josefina's shoulder. "Almost everyone in the village is healthy, praise God."

"Except for Doña Felícitas," Josefina reminded her. Elderly Doña Felícitas was full of aches and pains.

"You can bring comfort to Doña Felícitas," Tía Magdalena said firmly. Then she turned to the family servant who had accompanied them out to the open hills near Josefina's family *rancho,* watchful for any sign of trouble. "Miguel? Let's start back."

They headed toward the rancho through dusty hills glowing pink in the afternoon light. Mounds of rabbit brush bloomed with golden flowers, and the air smelled of *piñón* pine. When they neared the river, the water sang over the rocks in its path. Josefina let the beauty ease her worry. Since she'd started roaming with Tía Magdalena, Josefina had begun to understand the land's secrets.

Tía Magdalena continued her lessons. "That plant there—you know that one, *sí*?"

"Yarrow," Josefina said promptly. She touched the flower stalk, its tiny white blossoms now dry and brittle. "It's used for easing burns."

"Sí. And for love charms."

Josefina grinned at her godmother. "I remember you talking about that!"

"Lovelorn young women believe it's potent," Tía Magdalena said. "Especially if plucked from a young man's grave."

Josefina's smile faded as she wondered if her second-oldest sister, Francisca, knew about yarrow. These days, Francisca seemed to think more about getting married than anything else. She'd also grown impatient with the time Josefina spent learning about healing... but Josefina didn't want to spoil this lovely walk by thinking about the tension blooming between her and Francisca. Surely even Tía Magdalena couldn't cure that ailment.

They had walked farther from home than usual, but when Josefina spotted a huge flat rock perched on top of a narrow column she knew she was back on familiar ground.

"Not too far now," Josefina said. "There's Balancing Rock."

Tía Magdalena paused, leaning against a boulder. "My child, do you see that opening among the rocks?" She pointed with her walking stick at the cliffs near the river. "I'd like you and Miguel to go inside and look for *agua piedra*. You remember what it looks like?"

Josefina nodded. The powder ground from the unusual long, narrow stones sometimes helped people with stomach aches.

Josefina and Miguel left Tía Magdalena resting and scrambled up the gully. Miguel made Josefina wait in the sunshine while he checked below the overhanging rock for snakes and other dangers. "It's fine," he told her a few moments later. "You go in. I'll stay outside where I can also see your aunt."

"*Gracias.*" She gave Miguel a warm smile.

She always felt safe when he was near.

The cave's cool shadows felt good on Josefina's skin as she stepped inside and let her eyes adjust to the dim light. The cave was no bigger than one of the rooms in her rancho. She walked around, poking among the loose rocks with her toes. She didn't see anything that resembled the special stones Tía Magdalena wanted.

As Josefina walked back toward the sunshine, a striped lizard darted past. Watching it disappear, she noticed something else, almost hidden in the shadows. "Miguel," she called. "Come see."

"Señorita?"

"Someone has scratched the letter *S* in the rock wall." Josefina traced the letter with her fingers. "And here, below, is a cross."

Miguel peered at the markings. "It looks like a brand."

"Do you recognize it?" Josefina asked. Local ranchers used unique marks to identify their cattle.

"No, señorita." He shrugged. "A traveler must have left his mark here."

"But why would someone do that?" Josefina asked. "Doesn't it make you curious? It's some kind of secret sign!"

"Perhaps someone left a symbol of his faith," Miguel suggested. He cocked his head toward the cave opening. "Come, señorita. We should rejoin your aunt."

Josefina traced the rough markings with her finger again before turning to follow Miguel. What had the carver been trying to say? It was exciting to imagine that someone had left a sign, perhaps many years ago, that she could still see and touch! "Maybe that letter and cross were carved by a priest who found shelter here," she said. "Maybe it was one of the very first priests to come to New Mexico!"

"It's possible," Miguel agreed. "Back when many priests came to this area. Not like now." He sighed sadly.

Josefina tested the tippiness of a rock before stepping onto it, then nodded. Many priests had returned to Spain in the five years since Mexico had won independence. Now, instead of having their own village priest to say Mass for them every Sunday, Josefina's family and neighbors had to rely on a traveling priest who visited only a few times each year.

Josefina wanted to bring a smile back to Miguel's face. "Perhaps the marks were left by someone who buried treasure at that spot!" she teased. Everyone in New Mexico had heard countless tales of gold buried or lost in these hills.

"I'd need more than a cross scratched into a rock to convince me that I should dig for lost gold," Miguel said. "If God wants me to find buried treasure, I hope He will send me a map!"

Josefina laughed. She and Miguel joined Tía Magdalena, and the three headed for home.

❉

When Josefina followed Tía Magdalena through the small door cut into the huge front gate of her *adobe* home, she saw her sisters sitting in the courtyard making strings of onions. Her oldest sister Ana's two young sons played nearby while the young women braided the long green onion tops together. The strings would hang in the kitchen until the onions were needed for cooking. Clara and Ana greeted them warmly, but Josefina saw annoyance flicker in Francisca's eyes. "I'll come back and help as soon as we take care of the plants we collected," Josefina promised.

In the storeroom where Josefina kept the plants and roots used for dyes and *remedios*, she helped Tía Magdalena tie that day's harvest into bundles. "I enjoyed our walk," Tía Magdalena said when the last bunch was hanging from a rafter to dry. "I think I'll rest now, however."

Josefina hurried back to the courtyard and sat down near the remaining loose onions, newly dug and fragrant. "It's so nice to have you visiting," Josefina told Ana. Ana's family had moved to Santa Fe the previous spring to help tend Abuelito and Abuelita's rancho.

Francisca raised her eyebrows. "It's certainly nice for *some* of us to have Ana here. Clara and I couldn't have managed all these onions by ourselves while *you* were out roaming."

"We could have managed," Clara pointed out. "It just would have taken longer."

Josefina reached for several onions so that she could start her own braid. "Tía Magdalena is teaching me about important plants," she said quietly. "I need to know these remedios so that I can be a curandera one day."

Francisca's long sigh suggested that her fingers were worn to the bone with onion-braiding. "You're spending more time than ever with Tía Magdalena these days, just as everything in the garden is coming ripe."

Josefina felt a spring of hurt feelings bubble inside. "Every plant needs to be harvested at the particular time when it has the most power," she tried to explain. "Most remedies are best gathered now, in the autumn, when the full strength has come into the plants."

Francisca looked unconvinced. Josefina was grateful when Ana's sons, Antonio and Juan, chose that moment to get into a squabble. "Mamá," Juan howled. "Antonio—"

"Hush!" Ana scolded. "Tía Magdalena is resting. Do you wish to disturb her with your quarrels?"

Teresita, one of the family's servants, carried a basket brimming with more onions into the courtyard. "*Señora*, if you wish, I'll take the boys outside," she told Ana. "They can run and play."

Ana hesitated, then nodded. "Sí, *por favor*, Teresita." She gave her sons a firm look. "But you boys must promise to be good."

"Sí, Mamá." Juan headed toward the front gate.

"Juan!" Ana called sharply. "Listen to me. Obey Teresita, don't get too close to the water, and be back before the sun begins to set. You don't want to meet *La Llorona*, do you?"

11

That stopped him. Like all children, Juan and Antonio had heard the tale of La Llorona, the ghost of a long-ago woman whose children had drowned. Some people said that La Llorona still wandered about in the dark, weeping for her lost son and daughter. Josefina knew Ana wasn't trying to frighten her children—she was using the legend to remind her energetic sons to stay a safe distance from the creek and not wander away.

"I promise, Mamá," Juan said, looking sober, and Antonio nodded vigorously. Ana gave them each a kiss and sent them along with Teresita.

Francisca stared crossly at the basket of onions. "Oh! I am tired of nothing but chores, chores, chores."

"It wasn't 'chores, chores, chores' when Papá took us to Santa Fe last week," Josefina reminded her.

Ana gave Francisca a teasing smile. "I seem to remember a *fandango* you enjoyed there."

"And a certain young man who asked you

to dance—again!" Clara added.

Francisca's sigh this time was dreamy, not annoyed. "Oh, sí . . . Ramón Torres. He's asked me to dance several times since we were introduced last spring."

"What is he like?" Josefina asked.

A little smile tugged at Francisca's mouth. "He's *very* handsome," she said.

"Francisca?" Ana tipped her head. "Has Ramón Torres perhaps stolen your heart? Are you hoping he will ask Papá if he can come calling?"

"I don't know if Ramón's parents would permit him to court me." Francisca's fingers stilled in her lap. "His family is very well-to-do. Papá is a successful rancher, but we aren't as wealthy as the Torres family."

Josefina, Clara, and Ana exchanged glances. Beautiful Francisca had already attracted more than one suitor. Was she truly interested in Ramón Torres?

Francisca gazed away, and Josefina guessed that she wasn't seeing the flat adobe walls along the courtyard. "If only I could have some new clothes before the next fandango! I need a new dress, and a new silk *rebozo*. And perhaps a gold filigree necklace."

A frown crinkled Ana's forehead. "A silk rebozo won't ensure a good marriage," she said. "You need to know how to run a busy household. And you should choose a husband for his good heart, not just his good looks."

"I suppose you're right," Francisca said, shrugging sadly. "Still, some new finery would show Ramón's parents that I'm good enough for their son."

"Of course you're good enough for their son!" Clara said indignantly, but Josefina noticed Ana's worried silence.

Francisca wiped some dust from an onion and got back to work. "Well, I enjoy dancing with Ramón. We'll see if his parents write to Papá about a possible courtship." She glanced at Josefina. "If I married a wealthy man, I wouldn't have to do so much work!"

Josefina bit her lip. She'd do almost anything to make Francisca happy, but she couldn't give up her dream of being a curandera. She *would* keep learning from Tía Magdalena!

Still, Josefina hated the trouble simmering between her and Francisca. She remembered the longing in Francisca's eyes as she spoke of Ramón Torres. How wonderful it would be to present Francisca with a fancy silk shawl or gold necklace to wear at the next fandango! Such finery would surely impress Señora Torres—and the gift might smooth away Francisca's resentment.

Then Josefina sighed, flicking away a bit of papery onion skin. She had no money! She shouldn't even dream of giving Francisca an expensive gift.

Men's voices drifted into the courtyard. Papá and Miguel were coming in for their evening meal. Josefina remembered laughing as Miguel spoke of buried gold. *I shouldn't have laughed,* Josefina thought sadly.

2
TWO STRANGERS

The next morning, Josefina, Clara, and Francisca said good-bye to Ana as her husband Tomás harnessed their horses. A breeze nipped at Josefina's skin, but the autumn sky was a brilliant blue, and the yellow leaves of the cottonwood trees lining the stream nearby glowed in the early sun.

"It was wonderful to see you all!" Ana exclaimed.

"Couldn't you stay a little longer?" Josefina asked wistfully. "The Aragóns are having a harvest *fiesta* in the village tomorrow night." She was looking forward to the party. Everyone would help husk corn or slice apples, but many hands—and lots of songs and stories— would make the work pass quickly.

TWO STRANGERS

Ana smiled gently as she squeezed Josefina's hand. "We must return to Santa Fe."

Tía Dolores and Papá emerged from the house with Tía Magdalena. The curandera handed Tomás her traveling bag, then drew Josefina aside. "Don't worry so, my child!" she said, once again seeming to see into Josefina's heart. "I won't be away for long."

"Tía Magdalena," Josefina said, "did you always know you were meant to be a curandera? Even when you were young?"

Her aunt considered. "I always knew I was different from the other girls," she said finally.

"Did it make the others resent you?" Josefina bit her lower lip.

"Perhaps." Tía Magdalena smiled. "But in time I proved myself."

That's what I must do, Josefina thought. Perhaps God had given her this chance, while Tía Magdalena traveled, to prove herself!

Papá kissed Ana and her boys, and gave them his blessing before the travelers departed. Josefina felt a lingering shadow of sadness as she waved farewell. Then a warm hand squeezed her shoulder. "It was good to have them here, wasn't it?" Tía Dolores said softly. "I'll miss them, too."

Tía Dolores had come to stay after her older sister, Josefina's mother, had died. Back then, it had seemed that no light would ever shine on the Montoya rancho again. But Tía Dolores had come and captured the hearts of everyone in the family—including Papá, who had married her last winter. Josefina still missed her *mamá,* and prayed for her every day. But Tía Dolores helped remind Josefina that happiness might be waiting just beyond worry or sadness.

"Tía Magdalena asked me to visit Doña Felícitas while she is gone," Josefina told Tía Dolores. "I'm not sure I know enough to help Doña Felícitas. Oh, Tía Dolores! I want to *prove* that I am meant to be a curandera!"

"Tía Magdalena has faith in you." Tía Dolores looked Josefina squarely in the eye. "And so do I! Now, come along, Josefina.

There's work waiting for us in the kitchen, and as the saying goes, 'the saints cry over lost time.'"

❋

Tía Dolores kept Josefina, Francisca, and Clara too busy to worry or bicker for the rest of the day. The three girls helped the servants dig beets from the kitchen garden and lug the year's first pumpkins into the kitchen to be sliced and dried.

When the afternoon shadows had lengthened across the courtyard, Francisca stopped and stretched. "I'll make the *tortillas* for the evening meal," she offered. "That job will give me a rest!"

Josefina eased a pumpkin to the floor carefully. "And I'll bring water from the stream," she offered. She fetched the empty water jar and headed through the courtyard. As she stepped outside, she wondered whether Ana's family and Tía Magdalena had reached Santa Fe yet.

Then she squinted into the late afternoon sun. Someone was riding on horseback toward the rancho. No, two people.

Josefina darted back inside. Spanish priests were not the only people who had left New Mexico five years ago. Many of the soldiers had gone back to Spain, too. Now there were more incidents of bandits and raiders causing trouble.

She found her papá with Miguel, inspecting a harness that needed repair. "Papá!" she called breathlessly. "Two riders are approaching the rancho. I don't recognize them."

"Wait inside," Papá instructed calmly, dusting his hands on his trousers. "I'll meet our visitors. Miguel, come with me."

By the time the strangers neared the rancho, Josefina, Francisca, and Clara were pressed near the high, barred window in the front storeroom, which overlooked the road. "Come away, girls," Tía Dolores called from the kitchen. "It's impolite to stare like frightened prairie dogs."

Francisca dared a last peek out the window.
"One of the men is slumped over, as if he's
sick or hurt," she whispered. "I think the other
one is an *americano.*"

An americano! Josefina exchanged a surprised glance with Clara. They had met a
number of americanos—English-speaking men
who brought caravans of covered wagons full
of trade goods from the United States. Papá
had done business with them. Abuelito, an
experienced trader, had even traveled all the
way to Missouri and back with some of the
americanos. But Josefina had seen americanos
only in Santa Fe.

"Dolores!" Papá's shout drifted through
the window. "We need your help."

Josefina and her sisters followed Tía
Dolores toward the front gate just as Miguel
led the two horses into the courtyard. The
americano, who looked no older than Ana,
dismounted and helped Papá ease the second
man from his saddle. "Gracias," the americano
said in badly accented Spanish. His hair was

the color of ripe wheat. Hours spent outdoors had tanned his skin.

The injured man's hair was black, his skin the color of tea. His trousers and *sarape* looked as dusty as a field worker's after a hard day of harvest. His boots looked hard-used as well, although he seemed unable to put much weight on his left leg. A blood-stained bandage, perhaps made from his shirt, was tied just below the knee. "My name is Pedro Zamora," he gasped in a voice tight with pain. "I am a *rastreador,* seeking a chestnut mare. Her owner does not know if the horse is lost or was stolen. I—"

"Por favor, take him into the spare sleeping *sala,*" Tía Dolores interrupted, putting aside the polite introductions. Señor Zamora's eyes closed, and he would have slumped to the ground if the americano and Papá hadn't supported him.

Tía Dolores shooed the men forward with a wave of her hand. "Francisca and Clara," she said over her shoulder, "go back to the kitchen and help finish our meal. Josefina, come with me."

Josefina's stomach made a fist. *Oh, Tía Magdalena,* she thought. *I wish you were here.*

"Wait here a moment," Tía Dolores instructed Josefina when they reached the doorway of the sala. Then she followed the americano and Papá as they helped Señor Zamora inside.

Josefina tried to imagine how the stranger might have injured himself. He was a rastreador—a tracker. Rancho owners sometimes hired such trackers if valuable horses or cattle went missing. Why was he traveling with an americano?

A few moments later Tía Dolores reappeared. "Señor Zamora cut his leg," she told Josefina in a low tone. "The wound is beginning to fester, and he has a fever. Has Tía Magdalena taught you anything about such injuries?"

Josefina closed her eyes, thinking hard. "Safflower," she said after a moment. "An

ointment made from safflower and butter
will help keep wounds clean. Teresita uses
safflower to make a yellow dye! We might
have some on hand."

Tía Dolores nodded. "I believe Teresita is
in the weaving room. Run and ask her."

Josefina started to turn away but then
remembered something else. "Safflower petals,
boiled into stew, are good for strengthening
the heart," she added. "We have some mutton
stew left from the noon meal that we can heat
up for Señor Zamora."

Tía Dolores flashed Josefina an approving
smile. "Very good."

Josefina felt a flush of pride as she went
looking for Teresita. Sometimes she felt as if
all the plants and remedios Tía Magdalena
had told her about were whirling in her
memory like grains of sand in a dust storm.
She'd wondered if she would ever be able to
remember the right thing at the right time. But
safflower was a good remedio for a festering
wound, she was sure of it.

Two Strangers

To Josefina's relief, Teresita had a large bunch of safflower tucked away. Teresita was Navajo and had learned to dye yarn and weave blankets many years earlier, as a young girl. That was before she became a *cautiva*, someone stolen from her people by enemies, and was sold as a servant. Teresita had taught Josefina how to weave, and as Josefina had come to share Teresita's interest in useful wild plants, the two had developed a special relationship.

After they prepared the ointment, Josefina carried the bowl and clean bandages to the spare sala. "May I come in?" she called.

"Sí, Josefina," said Tía Dolores, beckoning.

Josefina stared at Señor Zamora, who was tucked into bed like a child. His forehead glistened with sweat, and he was mumbling under his breath. "What is he saying?"

Tía Dolores shook her head. "He's not making sense. That can happen with high fevers. Will you fetch more water, please? I'll have his leg bandaged by the time you return."

Josefina saw Señor Zamora's face in her mind as she hurried to the stream with a water jar. She had been worried about tending Doña Felícitas in the village—and now a patient with more serious problems had appeared! Had the mysterious stranger been sent to test her skill and knowledge?

As Josefina returned to the sala, she heard Tía Dolores talking to Señor Zamora in a soothing tone. "Your things are safe here, señor."

"Is his mind clearer?" Josefina asked, putting the water jar by the bed.

Tía Dolores shook her head. "Not really. He seems to be worried about his clothes." She gestured to a pile by the door. "Miguel provided our guest with a clean shirt to wear."

"We should put a damp cloth on his forehead," Josefina said. "That will help bring his fever down."

"You go ahead," Tía Dolores said. "I need to make sure that dinner preparations are well in hand, since we do have another guest! I'll return in a moment."

Josefina poured water into a bowl, wrung out a cloth, folded it neatly, and draped it over her patient's forehead. His eyes opened for a moment, as if he was startled by the coolness. "Señorita?" he whispered.

"My name is Josefina."

Señor Zamora clutched her arm with unexpected strength. "Por favor—where is my sarape?"

"Right over there." Josefina waved her hand toward the pile of clothes. "Don't worry, señor. With God's help, you will soon be well."

His hand fell back to the blanket, and his eyes flickered closed. Josefina touched the damp cloth and found it already warm. She replaced the cloth with another, and Señor Zamora began to murmur again. "The search... I must continue my search..."

"No, señor," Josefina told him quietly. "Your search for the horse can wait."

His head turned from side to side. "The rock," he muttered. "I found the rock."

Josefina bit her lip. "Please, señor," she begged. "Try to rest."

Teresita entered the sala, her quiet calm as comforting as Tía Dolores's brisk efficiency. "Your aunt asked me to sit with him," she told Josefina. "How is he?"

"Not well," Josefina said, regarding their visitor.

Teresita gave Josefina a reassuring smile that lit her whole face. "Don't worry, Señorita Josefina. If God wills it, our guest will recover."

Josefina nodded. She'd done what she could for Señor Zamora.

As she left the sala, she carried his dirty sarape out to the courtyard. It was too late in the day to launder his filthy shirt and trousers, but she could at least shake the dust from his sarape. It had once been of good quality, woven well of yellow and blue and red wool, but Josefina had trouble seeing the pattern through the dirt.

She gripped the woven cloak by the edge and gave it a hard, snapping shake. A cloud of dust billowed into the air. And something white fluttered to the ground.

Josefina stooped to pick up the piece of paper. It was thin, stained, and tattered. Three sides of the paper were cut straight. The fourth was ragged, as if this piece had come from a larger piece of paper that had been torn in two.

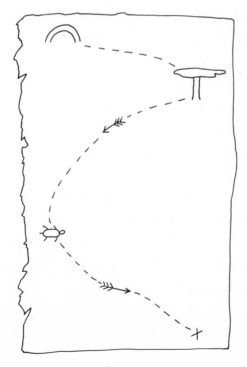

Squinting at the faded ink, Josefina made out an outline that looked familiar: a tall column supporting a flat surface. *That looks like Balancing Rock!* she thought. Was *that* the rock Señor Zamora had been speaking of? She tried to make out the other faint sketches: arrows, a turtle, curved lines that looked like a rainbow—

A burst of conversation from the kitchen interrupted Josefina's study, and her cheeks grew warm. This paper didn't belong to her! Taking a closer look at Señor Zamora's sarape, she found that he had stitched a small piece of thin hide to the inside of the cloak, making a hidden pocket. The map must have fallen from that pocket when she shook the sarape.

Clara appeared at the kitchen door. "Josefina? We're ready for the evening meal."

"Coming!" Josefina called. She slipped the fragile map carefully back into the sarape's hidden pocket, gently brushed what dust she could from the cloak, and folded it in such a way that the pocket—and the map

it contained—lay flat. Then she returned
the sarape to the sala. She would wash the
other clothes tomorrow, and whenever Señor
Zamora was ready to be on his way, he would
find his map just where he had left it.

But tucking the map away couldn't erase
it from Josefina's mind. She remembered
Miguel's reaction to the cross scratched into
the cave wall: "If God wants me to find buried
treasure, I hope He will send me a map!"

Señor Zamora had told Miguel that he'd
been searching for a missing mare. Yet his map,
old as it was, had surely not been drawn to
show him where to look for a horse! He was
searching for something else, she was sure of it.
Something secret. So . . . what was he seeking?

3

LA LLORONA

Josefina entered the main sala, where
the meal had been spread, just as Papá was
introducing his family to the americano.
"And this is my youngest daughter, Josefina,"
Papá said with a quiet pride that made
Josefina feel warm inside.

"Buenos días," the young americano said
carefully.

Josefina swallowed a smile as she folded
her hands and bowed her head politely. She
could tell that the stranger was trying hard
to speak proper Spanish, but since it was
evening, he should have said *"Buenas tardes."*

"This is Señor Roger Rexford," Papá told
Josefina. "He brought a letter of introduction
from your abuelito."

"Sí, I consider Señor Romero a friend," the americano added. "He sends his greetings from Santa Fe."

"*Bienvenido*, Señor Ro-ger Rex-ford," Josefina said, keeping her gaze courteously downcast. His English name was as hard for her to pronounce as some of the Spanish words were for him!

"My wife will make sure your friend is resting well before she joins us," Papá said. He gestured at the food steaming in serving dishes on the table. "Por favor, Señor Rexford, I hope you will honor us by joining us for our evening meal."

Roger Rexford bowed his head. "Gracias, Señor Montoya. The honor is mine." He took the place Papá indicated. Clara nudged Josefina and raised her eyebrows approvingly: *This americano knows his manners.* They had met nice americanos in Santa Fe but had also seen loud trappers, rude soldiers, and greedy traders who seemed to care nothing for Spanish customs.

"Señor Montoya," Señor Rexford said, "one thing I must explain. I don't know Señor Zamora. I came upon him as I made my way this afternoon. I could see he was"— he paused, searching for the word—"hurt, sí? So I brought him here for help."

"Ah." Papá nodded. "We will talk with Señor Zamora when he is stronger."

Good, Josefina thought. She wanted to know more about Señor Pedro Zamora! For now, she contented herself with stealing glances at the americano. Squinting into sunshine had created a tiny fan of lines at the corner of each eye, which crinkled when he grinned—as he did when Francisca passed him a bowl. "Ah," he sighed happily. He helped himself to a blue corn tortilla, topped it with layers of beans, chopped onion, yellow goat cheese, and lettuce, and then spooned red chile sauce on top. "This looks wonderful."

"You are accustomed to Mexican cooking, señor?" Papá asked.

"Sí, I am." The young man nodded vigorously. "I've been traveling the Santa Fe Trail for four years. That's how I met your abuelito," he added to the girls. Then he jumped to his feet as Tía Dolores appeared in the doorway.

"Buenas tardes," Tía Dolores said, taking her own place. "Por favor, continue your meal. Señor Zamora took a few spoonfuls of broth. Teresita is sitting with him."

Papá and Tía Dolores chatted with Señor Rexford while they finished their meal. He told funny stories about his adventures driving teams of mules on the Santa Fe Trail. Josefina understood why her abuelito had befriended this young man.

After dinner, Josefina was delighted when Tía Dolores asked Carmen, their cook, to make a pot of chocolate. Tía Dolores ordered cocoa beans from Mexico City every year and ground the beans with pecans, cinnamon, and a bit of sugar.

"Gracias," Señor Rexford said, accepting a

cup of the foamy treat. "Señor Romero told me that I would find a warm welcome in your home."

"You are indeed welcome," Papá said, "although I am curious why you are traveling alone." Now that dinner had been served, he was ready to discuss more serious topics. "The letter from my father-in-law says you have business to discuss?"

Josefina tried to hide her surprise. What business could this americano have with Papá?

"My father was the best saddle maker in Missouri," Señor Rexford began. "He taught me well."

Papá sat up a little straighter. Like many Mexican men, Papá was an excellent horseman.

Señor Rexford took another sip of chocolate. "When my father died, I had to sell his shop to settle some debts. My mother had died when I was small, so I was on my own. I signed on to pack and drive mules with a trade caravan because the leaders wanted someone who could repair harnesses and trappings along the way. I planned to save money and return one day to St. Louis—that's in Missouri—and open my own saddle shop." Señor Rexford smiled. "But a muleteer doesn't earn much money. I realized I needed another plan."

Papá leaned back in his chair. "And you have this new plan in mind?"

"Well, sir, I'm working on it." Señor Rexford looked half humble and half determined, and at that moment Josefina decided she liked him. "I'm thinking about setting up a saddle shop in Santa Fe for a few years. Just long enough to earn what I need to head back home."

Papá frowned slightly. "As you surely know, señor, trade regulations here are very complicated. You would need a trading license to go into business, and only Mexican citizens can obtain those licenses."

"Sí." Señor Rexford nodded. "But Americans *can* work here if they enter a partnership with a New Mexican." He grinned. "When my caravan arrived in Santa Fe, I visited my old friend Señor Romero. After much conversation, Señor Romero and I are considering going into business together."

Josefina hid a tiny smile. Her abuelito loved new adventures!

"I see," Papá said, exchanging a look with Tía Dolores. "But I'm still not sure why my father-in-law sent you here."

"Señor Romero suggested that I ask your advice about the rancho owners outside of Santa Fe," the young man explained. "Do you think they would be willing to order harnesses and saddles from an americano?"

Papá considered. "American saddles are quite different from Spanish saddles," he said. "I don't know if men will make the change."

"I have studied Spanish saddles," Señor Rexford said. He leaned forward eagerly, his elbows on his knees. "I have great admiration for the workmanship I've seen. I want to blend features from different styles of saddles to create something even more useful and beautiful."

For a long moment no one spoke. Then Papá said, "I'll think about that idea. Let's talk more tomorrow."

✽

After prayers that evening, Tía Dolores checked on Señor Zamora while Josefina waited outside. When Tía Dolores emerged, she said softly, "He's sleeping. Go on to bed, Josefina. I've asked one of the servants to sit with him."

I'm glad someone is sitting with Señor Zamora, Josefina thought, turning toward her sleeping sala. She felt uneasy about their mysterious guest. He had probably lied about being a rastreador searching for a missing horse. For a moment Josefina regretted not telling Tía Dolores about the map she'd found—but her cheeks burned at the idea of admitting she'd looked at a paper that didn't belong to her. More importantly, she didn't know that Señor Zamora had done anything wrong.

Josefina considered confiding in Clara and

Francisca, but when she found them whispering excitedly about Roger Rexford as they unrolled their sleeping pallets, she dismissed that idea, also. Francisca had been too impatient with her lately, and practical Clara would probably think Josefina's unease was silly. No, Señor Zamora's map was better kept a secret.

"I can tell Señor Rexford misses St. Louis," Clara was saying. "Abuelito says it's an exciting place."

Francisca smoothed a blanket impatiently. "Who cares about St. Louis?" she asked. "I don't. Santa Fe is big enough for me."

Clara and Josefina traded knowing looks. "And of course," Clara teased softly, "a certain handsome and wealthy young man lives in Santa Fe."

"I can dream, can't I?" Francisca asked simply. She slid under her blanket and turned to face the wall.

Josefina sighed. Once she had thought that having Tía Dolores marry Papá was all the sisters needed to keep life in balance. But things kept changing! *I can't make Ramón Torres decide to call on Francisca,* she thought. *But I still wish I had some way of giving Francisca a beautiful gift to help impress his parents.*

Long after Francisca and Clara were asleep, Josefina twisted and tossed beneath her blanket. Her mind turned from Señor Rexford, who seemed so nice, to the mysterious Señor Zamora. Was he resting comfortably? Had she made the correct recommendation to Tía Dolores? Josefina had been *sure* of her choice at the time. Now, the night's dark stillness gave room to creeping doubts.

And who *was* Señor Zamora? What was he looking for? Was it . . . could it truly be some kind of treasure? Was he an honest man? Perhaps he was a bandit, returning to recover treasure he'd stolen from good, hardworking people!

Josefina had grown up hearing tales of treasures hidden by thieves, gold mines with secret entrances, jars of coins buried by old men afraid of being robbed. She'd always enjoyed these legends, shared by good storytellers when shadows were long and imaginations ran high. She'd never heard of anyone actually finding lost treasure. But she'd never seen a map marked with land-marks and strange sketches, either.

Josefina tried to push the image of the map from her mind so that she could go to sleep, but it was no use. Finally, afraid she might wake her sisters, she got up. Wrapping her rebozo around her shoulders against the cool night breeze, she tiptoed out of the sala. She lit a candle and crept to the storeroom where she and Teresita kept their remedios and dyes.

Josefina loved the musty-spicy smells of the plant bundles hanging from poles over-head. She loved seeing bins and gourds and baskets filled with supplies that might help ward off illness or cure disease. Sitting on a *banco,* she savored the peaceful stillness. She could feel her muscles relaxing. Soon she would be ready for sleep.

Then an unexpected sound jerked Josefina upright. The candle fell to the hard earthen floor and snuffed out. In the sudden darkness, Josefina strained to hear the sound that had disturbed her. There it was again! A faint crying sound.

Was one of her sisters awake? Was Francisca in the courtyard, weeping for Ramón? Josefina cocked her head, but when she heard the sound again, she was sure it came from *outside* the house.

Josefina stepped closer to the window, carefully avoiding a basket of pumpkin stems. Pressing a palm against the wall, she held her breath. And the sound came again, drifting through the open window above her head— a woman's sob, low and full of anguish.

Josefina's bones turned to ice. Only one woman roamed at night, weeping and wailing: the ghost, La Llorona!

4
A FRIGHTENING PREDICTION

"Wake up, sleepy!" Clara shook Josefina's shoulder. "Usually I only have to push Francisca out of bed!"

Josefina blinked and rubbed her eyes. Soft morning light filled the girls' sleeping sala. "I'm awake," she mumbled, although it seemed as if only moments had passed since she'd fallen asleep. She had run back to bed after hearing La Llorona the night before, but sleep had been a long time coming.

"Good," Clara said, "because we have lots to do. Tía Dolores wants to bake bread today, and we need to check for ripe squashes, and—"

"And there's the harvest fiesta tonight in the village," Francisca added. She gave Josefina a hard look. "We need you to do your fair share of chores today, instead of wandering off somewhere to collect plants. Tía Dolores won't let us go to the village until we get our work done here."

"I'll do my part," Josefina retorted. She was tired of Francisca's pointed comments! And she was just plain *tired,* worn out by her nighttime worries. Was it possible that she *had* heard just a gust of wind, or an animal? Or had she really heard La Llorona?

Clara interrupted her thoughts. "Don't argue, por favor," she said quietly.

"I don't mean to argue," Josefina said, reaching for her shoes. "I didn't sleep well last night." She swallowed hard. "I got up in the night, and . . . and I thought I heard—"

"Oh!" Francisca interrupted, her voice full of frustration. "The embroidery on this blouse needs repair, and I want to wear it tonight! Clara, will you help me?"

"Let me see." Clara hurried over to inspect the damage. Josefina felt a flicker of loneliness as she watched her sisters finger the fabric.

Then she brightened. All the villagers would be together this evening. People would share news and tell stories. If anyone knew anything about a wandering woman, Josefina would surely hear about it. *And maybe,* she thought, *someone will tell a tale of buried gold or treasure maps.* It might be an interesting evening!

❈

After *siesta* that afternoon, Miguel escorted Tía Dolores and the girls to the village about a mile from their rancho. The road passed between fields and the stream. Leaves from the cottonwood trees drifted lazily toward the ground like bits of sunshine. Men picked corn in fields dotted with orange pumpkins.

Josefina's studies with Tía Magdalena had sharpened her awareness, and she took pride in noting that some branches on an alder tree near the stream had been stripped of bark. *Teresita must have been here,* she thought. She felt rewarded when an unexpected flash of color caught her eye. She stepped from the road and pulled a thin band woven of red, yellow, and orange yarn from the lower branches of a sumac bush.

"What did you find?" Tía Dolores called.

"One of Teresita's hair cords." Josefina displayed her find before putting it into the small leather pouch she wore at her waist. Teresita wore her hair in an unusual twist at the back of her head and used the colorful cords to tie it in place. "She must have been collecting alder bark to dye wool."

"God has granted us a good harvest in many ways," Tía Dolores said, and smiled.

They soon arrived at the village. The church, the largest building, seemed to watch over the low adobe houses like a kind shepherd. The houses surrounded a tidy *plaza*, with gardens and goat pens and chicken coops behind them. Josefina felt as at home in the village as she did at the rancho. She'd played games with other children in the plaza, celebrated holidays in the church, and attended gatherings in peoples' homes during times of sadness and joy.

When they entered the plaza, Josefina saw two men tossing ears of corn from a wagon, making huge piles in front of the Aragón home. Josefina's friend Ofelia Aragón stepped outside with a basket of apples. "Buenas tardes!" she called, waving. Her parents were hosting the harvest fiesta.

"I hope you've hidden a watermelon under all that corn," Josefina said. "When the husking is finished, we'll deserve a reward!"

"Sí, of course!" Ofelia's eyes danced, and Josefina laughed. Ofelia always found joy in whatever the day brought: a sweet bird call, a beautiful sunset, a gathering of friends.

"I'll be back soon," Josefina promised Ofelia. Then she took Tía Dolores's hand. "May I visit Doña Felícitas?"

Tía Dolores walked Josefina to the widow's house. "I'll come back to fetch you later," she said, and gave Josefina an encouraging nod.

Doña Felícitas lived in a tired adobe house near the church. Josefina knocked on the door, then eased it open. "Buenas tardes, Doña Felícitas. It's me, Josefina Montoya."

"Josefina? Come in." Doña Felícitas waved Josefina inside with a cupped hand. The widow was a tiny woman with a face as wrinkled as a plum left too long in the sun. She sat hunched near her fireplace, wrapped in layers of rebozos. "Is Magdalena with you? I need her help."

Josefina set down the basket of remedios she'd brought. "Tía Magdalena went to Santa Fe," she reminded Doña Felícitas. "How are you feeling?"

Doña Felícitas's voice quavered. "My hands and knees ache. I was hardly able to fix myself a bite to eat this morning."

Josefina looked around the room. It needed a good sweeping and dusting, and the wood-box was empty. "Perhaps you should consider getting a servant to help you, señora," she said.

"If only I could," Doña Felícitas lamented. "But I have all I can do to keep food on my own table. I have no money for such help."

"Of course," Josefina murmured, sorry that

she'd made the suggestion. She knew Doña Felícitas was a widow and had no children or grandchildren to help her. Although the villagers kept an eye on her, making sure she always had food and firewood, it was a hard life for the old woman.

"If I had someone to help me, I could keep a better garden." The old woman turned her head away. "But a full garden would not help me today. My stomach hurts."

Josefina felt a moment of panic as she sat down by the widow. "I'm sorry to hear that."

"When I was a new bride, I kept the finest garden in the village." Doña Felícitas's voice sounded faraway. "I remember—"

"Pardon me," Josefina said as politely as she knew how. She hated interrupting, but she knew from experience that Doña Felícitas's stories were long and involved. "May I fix you a cup of tea, señora? Some mint tea might settle your stomach."

Josefina built up the fire, brought in extra wood, and brewed the widow a cup of tea.

Then she gently massaged Doña Felícitas's aching hands, just as Tía Magdalena had shown her, and applied a poultice made of *yerba mansa* leaves.

"You have no idea how I suffer," Doña Felícitas sighed, leaning back in her chair. "But one must suffer in order to earn grace."

Doña Felícitas's sadness filled her home like smoke from a poorly made fire. Tía Magdalena always managed to bring a little cheer to the widow. Josefina didn't know what to say or do to bring a smile to the old woman's face. Perhaps she should try to distract Doña Felícitas from her aches. "The Aragóns are having a harvest party this evening," Josefina began.

Doña Felícitas sighed again. "I used to go to such parties. Now I am confined to my house. When I was a girl . . ."

Josefina let Doña Felícitas's words flow around her. What else could she try? *I'll remind her that the priest is coming,* Josefina thought.

When the widow finally paused, Josefina said, "Next week we'll celebrate the fiesta of

San Francisco de Asís." San Francisco was the patron saint of their village church. "Padre Simón will come in time for the bonfires the night before the fiesta, and the next day he'll say our special Mass, and we'll have dancing and fireworks! If you sit by the window, you'll be able to see the morning procession and all the festivities."

"I wish I could still walk in the procession. I can't even go to the church." Doña Felícitas sounded more miserable than ever. "I have lost my greatest comfort."

"I can try to help you walk to the church for the fiesta," Josefina offered. "You're lucky that your house is so close."

"It would be too hard for me," Doña Felícitas said. "Oh, how I miss the days when we had our own priest in the village! Our old priest visited anyone who was sick, every day." She stared at the floor. "But things have been changing here for a long, long time. Even when I was your age, our church was not as beautiful as it once was. Did you know that a

beautiful cross once hung over the altar?
My abuelito told me that it was made by a
famous artist in Spain and brought to our
church. But back in 1680, when the Pueblo
Indians chased all the Spanish settlers out of
New Mexico, the priest took it with him to
keep it safe. The Spanish priests and soldiers
eventually came back, of course, but they didn't
bring our cross back with them."

Josefina thought about all the occasions
when her family and their neighbors had
gathered joyfully to clean or replaster their
church, or to embroider beautiful altar cloths,
or to decorate the sanctuary for feast days
and celebrations. Doña Felícitas seemed
determined to be unhappy even about their
church! Josefina didn't want to hear any more,
and she was relieved when she glanced out
the window and saw Tía Dolores approaching.
"I'll visit again tomorrow," she promised, then
quickly made her escape.

❋

An hour later Josefina sat waist-deep in cornhusks beside Ofelia, enjoying the sound of laughter. After Josefina's mamá died, her family had known sadness as deep as Doña Felícitas's . . . but in time, they had opened their hearts to happiness again. Josefina was afraid that Doña Felícitas didn't know how to be happy any longer.

Tía Dolores sat with the married women, looping slices of apples on string to dry. Papá had joined the party too, and had brought Señor Rexford. They stood chatting with some of the other men. Francisca's fingers flew, pulling husks from the ears of corn, but her eyes sparkled as she talked with friends.

Josefina looked for Clara and finally spotted her near the house, talking with Ofelia's cousin Soledad. After Soledad's parents had died last spring, Soledad had come to the village and moved in with Ofelia's family. She was a lovely young woman, tall and graceful, but very shy. Clara was gesturing toward the huskers, as if inviting Soledad to join them. Soledad smiled but shook her head and disappeared into the house. A moment later she appeared with a tray of *bizcochitos* and began offering guests the sweet cookies.

"Doesn't Soledad want to sit with us?" Josefina asked Ofelia.

Ofelia glanced toward her cousin. "Soledad prefers to help in the kitchen," she said. "She's an excellent cook." She reached for another ear of corn. "How was your visit with Doña Felícitas?"

Josefina sighed. "Nothing I tried made her feel any better. I knew her bones ached, but she told me today that her stomach is also troubling her!"

Soledad appeared and offered her tray. "Na—" she began, then swallowed whatever she was going to say, looking embarrassed.

"Gracias, Soledad!" Josefina helped herself to a cookie and smiled encouragingly. Soledad returned a timid smile and turned away.

Ofelia was giving Josefina a sympathetic look. "Soon your Tía Magdalena will come home, and you won't have to worry so much about Doña Felícitas."

Josefina shrugged, frustrated. She wanted to help people herself. Surely she had learned enough to be able to provide some comfort to the elderly woman!

I did what I could today, she told herself. *Tomorrow I'll think of something else to try.*

❋

When a full harvest moon rose in the cloudless sky, parents carried their youngest children to bed. Then everyone settled in for storytelling. Josefina helped husk another basket's worth of corn before one of the older men told a tale about a rich man who had hidden his money in a hole in an old tree in his orchard, then couldn't remember which tree. Desperate to find the money, he'd chopped down all of his trees before realizing that someone must have watched him hide the coins and stolen them. "And so that man lost his coins *and* his orchard," the storyteller said.

Ofelia's mother smiled. "Wealth does not always bring happiness."

"Still, many dream of finding riches," a boy about Francisca's age said. "God sometimes rewards those who work hard. I've heard many stories about treasure in the hills."

Josefina's fingers stilled. She leaned closer.

"Empty tales," a man scoffed.

Another neighbor, Señor Sánchez, held up a hand in protest. "Perhaps, perhaps not. My abuelito told me that he thought people buried their gold before fleeing south during the Pueblo uprising."

Ofelia nudged Josefina. "Can you imagine finding buried treasure?" she whispered. "I'd buy a new guitar for Papá!"

"I'd buy a gold filigree necklace and a silk shawl for Francisca," Josefina whispered back. "And . . . and I'd pay for a servant to help Doña Felícitas!"

One of the men wasn't indulging in daydreams. "But why didn't people who buried their gold retrieve it when they came back?"

Señor Sánchez shrugged. "Who can say? Perhaps the people died before they *could* come back. Or perhaps they did return but couldn't remember exactly where they'd hidden it."

"If I buried treasure, I'd draw a map so that I couldn't forget the spot!" someone laughed.

Josefina pictured the map she'd found hidden in Pedro Zamora's sarape. What could he be searching for, if not lost treasure? Whatever it was, his search had been halted.

But... couldn't *she* search?

Josefina felt a ripple of excitement as she considered the idea. Whatever Señor Zamora was seeking must be *somewhere* near Balancing Rock. And if she found it, she might learn why Señor Zamora had lied about being a rastreador—and whether it was dangerous for Papá to let him recover under their roof!

But Josefina had no idea what the turtle and the rainbow meant. If someone had scratched those marks on rocks, it seemed unlikely that she could actually find them.

Still, there was no harm in looking for the symbols, was there?

Suddenly Josefina blinked, startled from her thoughts.

"Are you sure it was La Llorona that you heard?" Ofelia asked a boy named Marcos. The conversation had broken up again, and the adults were busy with their own discussion.

"Who else could it have been?" His voice was sober. "I'm telling you, I *heard* the Weeping Woman last night."

Josefina suddenly felt chilled. Someone else had heard crying in the night? The same night she'd heard it at her rancho?

"I remembered that I'd left a sickle in the field, and I went to get it so the blade wouldn't rust," Marcos was saying. "Then I heard La Llorona, crying softly for her lost children. I ran right back home!" He shivered. "Whenever La Llorona is heard weeping at night, a death is sure to follow!"

Josefina's chill settled in her bones, and her fingers seemed frozen to the corn. The

Weeping Woman had been heard on the very day Tía Magdalena left the village. Josefina had heard La Llorona at the rancho, where Señor Zamora was being treated for a bad leg wound; and Marcos had heard La Llorona near the village, where old Doña Felícitas was ailing.

Was the weeping an omen for the people in Josefina's care?

5

BEGINNING THE SEARCH

When Josefina stopped at Señor Zamora's doorway the next morning to look in on him, Teresita joined her. "His fever remains high," Teresita said in a low tone. "His wound is healing, though. Don't give up hope, señorita."

Josefina stared at Señor Zamora. His sun-lined face wore a faint frown, and his calloused hands twitched even in sleep. *Who are you?* she wanted to ask. *What are you searching for?* She couldn't help glancing at his neatly folded sarape, picturing his map in her mind.

Teresita picked up an empty bowl. "The señor took some mutton broth this morning. I'll take this back to the kitchen. He needs sleep more than anything else, now."

"Teresita, would you accompany me into the hills this afternoon?" Josefina asked. "If I can find some agua piedra, it might help Doña Felícitas. I'll ask Papá if he can spare Miguel."

"Sí, I would like that," Teresita said. "I need more rabbit brush for dyeing wool."

"Oh! That reminds me." Josefina reached for the pouch at her waist. "Have you dyed any wool with the alder bark you collected yet?"

Teresita looked confused. "I haven't collected any alder bark this year."

"But I found one of your hair ties near an alder tree by the river." Josefina pulled the colorful woven ribbon from her pouch.

Teresita accepted the tie, looked at it carefully, and tucked it away. "Of course you're right, señorita. I've had so much on my mind that I forgot."

Josefina frowned as the older woman turned away. Teresita must be more worried about Señor Zamora than she'd admitted.

❇

Aware of waiting chores, Josefina hurried to the courtyard. Tía Dolores, Francisca, and Clara were already sitting amid piles of the most colorful harvest of all, scarlet chile peppers. The brilliant peppers had cured in the courtyard sun for two days and were now ready to be made into long strings, which would be hung out of the way until needed.

Roger Rexford sat against one wall in the courtyard, mending a bridle. "Those peppers are very pretty," he said.

"And they taste good," Josefina added, as she sat down and picked up several chiles. "At least in small portions!" Chile peppers were too fiery to eat whole.

"There's a tree in Missouri called a 'maple,'" Señor Rexford told them. "We had one by our house that turned bright red in the fall. And if anyone had told me there was a prettier sight, I would have called him a liar. But those are..." He searched for an adequate Spanish word.

Tía Dolores smiled. "Cheerful? Bright? We call these strings of chiles *ristras*."

"New Mexico must be very different from what you are used to," Clara said.

"It feels like a different world," Señor Rexford admitted. "At first, it was hard to get used to all the—the *space*." The americano's eyes had a faraway look. "When I'm ready to settle down, I'm going to find a place with lots of big maple trees that turn red each year."

Josefina had never seen a maple tree, but she could tell it was something wonderful. "I hope your wish comes true, Señor Rexford," she said.

The americano smiled, then looked at Tía Dolores. "Por favor, Señora Montoya, I would like it if you all called me Roger."

Francisca giggled, then quickly coughed to cover her rude behavior. "New Mexican women do not take their husband's last name when they marry, as American women do," Tía Dolores explained. "I'm known as Señora Romero. As for your request, since you may be going into business with my father, I believe it would be all right."

"There must be many things to remember

when you travel in a new place," Josefina said, hoping the americano wasn't discouraged by his mistake.

"There are more things to learn than just a new language," Roger agreed. "But it's interesting to meet new people and see new places."

Francisca finished her first ristra and hung it against the adobe wall behind her, where the pepper pods gleamed in the sun. "I need to rest," she said, rubbing one hand with the other. "After a while, those peppers sting!"

"Let me give it a try." Roger put the bridle aside and joined them. "How do you start?"

Josefina could tell that Francisca was struggling not to laugh again. Americanos did have strange ideas sometimes! The sisters had never seen a mule driver string ristras before.

"Start with three chiles," Francisca said after she swallowed her giggles. "Toss away any with bad spots. Now, wrap a string around the stems like this..." After he'd secured the first chiles, Francisca showed Roger how to add more peppers to the string. "It's like braiding hair," she told him. "The string is one strand, and the stems of two chiles become the other two strands."

"Braiding?" Roger grinned as he tucked the new word into his memory. "I haven't braided much hair in my life. But I think I understand."

"How are your plans for a saddle shop progressing, Roger?" Tía Dolores asked.

"Gracias for asking." He paused, looking thoughtful. "Your husband has kindly introduced me to some of his friends. I'm learning what they look for in a good saddle."

"Do you think you and Abuelito can make a business succeed?" Josefina asked.

"I don't know," he admitted. "We'll talk more when I head back to Santa Fe in a couple of days."

"It's too bad you can't wait until next week!" Clara exclaimed. "We'll be celebrating the fiesta of San Francisco de Asís."

"I wish I could stay!" Roger said. "But my caravan will be leaving before too long. Your abuelito and I must decide whether I'm heading out with it, or setting up shop in Santa Fe."

"I hope you can follow your dream," Josefina said. "I hope you get your"—she found the strange word—"maple trees."

"Gracias." Roger gave her a warm smile.

❀

After the noon meal, Miguel escorted Josefina and Teresita as they set out for a hill where rabbit brush grew in cheerful abundance. After murmuring a prayer, Teresita began a careful harvest. "We must never take more plants than we can use," she reminded Josefina. "Gather some from each direction so that this patch stays balanced, and always leave some behind."

When Teresita was satisfied, Miguel led Josefina to several rocky overhangs. None contained the special stones she wanted. "I'll have to find another remedio for Doña Felícitas," Josefina said finally.

As they wound their way toward home,

Josefina kept the excursion pointed toward Balancing Rock. She walked slowly, her gaze searching every rock for any mark resembling a turtle or a rainbow. Out here, where the mesas and arroyos rippled endlessly away from her, finding a scratched symbol seemed as likely as finding a particular speck of cornmeal in an overflowing barrel.

"Miguel," she said when they stopped to refresh themselves from the canteen of water he carried. "Do you recall those marks we found last week—the S and cross?"

"Of course, señorita."

"Have you ever seen any other markings? Especially in this area, near Balancing Rock?" Josefina pointed to the towering formation.

Miguel smiled. "These hills are as familiar to me as my own hands, señorita. I know where someone long ago marked figures of two men, and another spot where a sun has been chipped into a rock wall. That one's hard to see, though. It's very old, and rain and wind have smoothed the marks."

I should have considered that, Josefina thought, her hopes sinking lower. If the person who made Señor Zamora's treasure map had scratched his symbols in haste, thinking he would soon be able to retrace his steps and reclaim the treasure, he probably hadn't made his marks very deep. Would he have been thoughtful enough to leave his signs in a sheltered spot? Had many years of storms worn the designs away altogether?

Josefina looked at Miguel. "Why do you think so many people have left secret signs among these hills?"

"Sometimes I can guess," Miguel told her. "I once found a coiled rattlesnake carved into a stone. Someone was surely warning travelers of a snake den. I stayed away!"

I don't want to stumble onto a rattlesnake! Josefina thought with a shudder. "Have you ever seen a mark like a turtle scratched into a rock? Or curved lines, like a rainbow?" she asked, and when Miguel shook his head, she turned to Teresita.

Teresita gave Josefina a searching look. "No, señorita."

Josefina felt a pang of disappointment so sharp that it surprised her. *Finding treasure was a nice daydream,* she thought. Had she truly expected to find treasure so easily? Or . . . had she only wanted to believe she could discover the treasure because she was starting to doubt whether she could provide any real aid to Doña Felícitas? It would be nice to solve at least one problem!

Josefina took one last look around her, imagining someone hiding treasure, desperate to secure it safely before bandits or raiders descended. The treasure might still be waiting, but in this vast open space, it was hard to believe that anyone could ever find it again.

❋

"Josefina, where have you been?" Francisca demanded when Teresita and Josefina returned to the rancho. "Clara and I had to haul all of the squash from the garden by ourselves."

Teresita took Josefina's collecting bag. "I'll take this to the storeroom for you," she murmured, then left the sisters alone.

"I was searching for a remedio for Doña Felícitas." A finger of guilt poked at Josefina's conscience, for if she hadn't wasted time searching for lost treasure, she would have been home earlier. "But I'll help you now."

"You won't be helping *me*." Francisca turned away. "I have a headache. I'm going to rest." Josefina's shoulders slumped as she watched Francisca disappear.

Josefina spent the rest of the afternoon weaving a blanket. Then she carried water from the stream and helped prepare the evening meal. By the time the final kitchen chores were done, she was tired and downhearted and ready for bed. Then she remembered the collecting bag she had given to Teresita. She'd forgotten to tend to the plants she'd collected! *Perhaps I can wait until tomorrow to sort and hang them?* she asked herself, but knew she could not. It wouldn't be respectful to leave the plants she'd gathered wilting in her bag.

Josefina slipped from the sala and crossed through the back courtyard, near the servants' quarters, to the storeroom. Then she carefully separated the plants she had gathered that day, tied them into bundles, and hung them from a pole overhead. *There,* she thought.

Shadows had darkened the room by the time Josefina finished. The back courtyard had become quiet too, as the servants completed their chores and settled down in their salas. Josefina stretched as she stepped out of the storeroom and started across the courtyard. Now she could go to bed with a clear conscience.

Then she heard a woman's voice—just a snatch, low and indistinct. It seemed to come from beyond the adobe walls. *It must be one of the servants,* she thought. But the only door from the back courtyard to the outdoors, just beyond the storeroom, was already closed for the evening.

The unhappy tone came again, then faded away. Josefina realized that it had drifted through one of the holes carved into a beam just below the roof, in a corner of the courtyard. The opening was a *golondrina* hole, made to encourage swallows inside to eat insects.

Then the woman's voice rose to a single soft wail, oddly muffled as it drifted through the golondrina hole. Josefina stiffened with sudden fear. *La Llorona!*

Josefina's heart beat too quickly as she tiptoed to the door. She unlatched it, gathered her courage, and poked her head into the twilight.

Something rustled into the shadows, then faded away.

Josefina waited for what seemed forever, willing the woman to return, to make her presence known, to weep or to wail or to state her intentions. Finally, with a flush of relief that made her knees tremble, Josefina locked the door against the night's secrets and hurried to bed.

6

A NEW PARTNERSHIP

After morning prayers the next day, as Clara and Francisca headed toward the kitchen, Tía Dolores put a hand on Josefina's arm. "Señor Zamora's fever has broken!" she said.

Josefina clasped her hands together. "The saints have smiled on us!"

"Señor Zamora won't be able to travel right away, though," Tía Dolores said. "It seems unlikely that he'll ever find the mare he was seeking."

"Sí." Josefina shifted her weight. The relief she felt drained away like rain in the desert as she remembered the map. Should she let Señor Zamora leave the rancho without telling Papá and Tía Dolores what she'd seen? Or should she admit that she'd examined one of their guest's belongings, even though she'd failed to discover what it meant?

Before Josefina could decide, Tía Dolores said, "I told Señor Zamora he could sit in the courtyard for a while this afternoon. He asked to speak with you. I think he wishes to thank you for your help." Although her tone was mild, a question seemed to hover in her eyes.

I'll learn why Señor Zamora wants to talk with me, Josefina thought. *Then I'll decide what to tell Tía Dolores and Papá.* "I think permitting our guest to sit in the courtyard is a fine idea," she said meekly. She was relieved when Tía Dolores nodded and turned toward the kitchen.

❉

Josefina and Teresita walked to the village after breakfast with unexpected company. "Gracias for escorting us," Josefina told Roger as they arrived in the plaza.

"I'm happy to!" the americano declared. "Señor Sánchez is going to show me a saddle. Why don't I meet you later in front of the

75

church?" When Josefina agreed, he walked away, whistling cheerfully.

As Josefina and Teresita passed the Aragón home, Ofelia called from the doorway, "Josefina!" She hurried outside and pressed a cloth-covered dish into Josefina's hands. "Mamá asked me to give you this," she said breathlessly. "We're grateful for your family's help at the harvest fiesta. I must go back inside now, but I'll see you tomorrow when we make decorations for San Francisco's feast day!"

"Sí," Josefina called back. "And gracias!"

As they turned away, Josefina peeked under the cloth. "Oh, bizcochitos! But . . . what's this?" She gently pulled out a single string that held half a dozen tiny bundles of dried herbs. Josefina brought one to her nose, breathing in its scent. "I think Tía Magdalena calls this *cota*."

Teresita had a strange expression on her face. She fingered the herbs, then sniffed the bundles as Josefina had. "*Ch'ilahwéhé.* My mother saved this plant in little bundles just like this and used them to make tea."

Josefina's eyes widened. Teresita almost never mentioned her childhood, and Josefina had never before heard her speak Navajo. "Teresita . . . do you still miss your mamá?"

Teresita looked away for a moment. "Many years have passed since I saw her. I still remember my mamá, and many of the things she taught me. I'm grateful for that. I'm also grateful for all the things I've learned since."

"I think it's that way for me, too," Josefina said slowly. "Mamá will always be a part of me. But I'm also thankful for everything Tía Dolores and Tía Magdalena have taught me. And you," she added. She was rewarded by Teresita's beautiful smile.

Teresita put the dried plants back into Josefina's hand. "Why did the señora give this to you?" she wondered.

Josefina thought back through her lessons with Tía Magdalena. "Cota is good for many things—especially stomach trouble." She looked at Teresita with delight. "This gift is very timely, since I wasn't able to find any agua piedra!" Josefina's burden of worry felt a little lighter. This quiet gesture of support from Ofelia's mother was *almost* like getting help from her own dear mamá.

As they reached the widow's home, Teresita said, "I'll see if there is any work to be done in Doña Felícitas's garden."

Josefina was sorry to find Doña Felícitas in bed. "I couldn't get up," the old woman said. "My knees ache so."

"Is your stomach still troubled?" Josefina asked.

"Oh, sí." Doña Felícitas patted Josefina's hand. "When I was a young girl, my little sister was often ill . . ."

"I brought something that might help," Josefina said before Doña Felícitas could detour the conversation too far. "I'll make you some tea."

Soon Josefina had the sala tidy, a cheerful fire burning in the hearth, and a cup of fragrant tea brewing. "Our servant Teresita is working in your garden," she told her patient.

"Gracias to you both, Josefina." The widow sighed. "But it does weigh on my heart to know that I can no longer manage on my own."

"Can you sit up, señora? By God's grace, this tea will help." Josefina arranged a pillow for Doña Felícitas and helped her sip some of the tea. "I had another idea," she added. "Some of us are going to make flower garlands for the saint's day celebration. May we gather here in your house? Then you can be part of the festivities!" She smiled. This was the best idea she'd had yet.

Doña Felícitas, though, waved one hand in feeble dismissal. "I don't think so, Josefina. I fear it would be too distressing."

"But..." Josefina struggled to understand. "We would appreciate your company, señora. And we wouldn't stay too long, or tire you."

"No." Doña Felícitas's voice was thin

but firm. "Two of my neighbors visited me yesterday. And what did they speak of? Nothing but La Llorona!"

Josefina's fingers began gathering her skirt into tiny folds. "La Llorona?"

"Several people have heard the Weeping Woman near the village," Doña Felícitas told her. "Señora López said she heard the crying, faint but clear. I've heard stories of La Llorona all my life, but I don't recall ever seeing people so upset."

La Llorona again! Josefina thought. A prickling sensation rippled over her skin, as if someone were tracing patterns with a dried stem of rabbit brush. The nighttime weeping couldn't be explained by the wind or a boy's imagination—not if people like sensible Señora López had heard it too. And the tales were clearly upsetting Doña Felícitas. Did the old woman sense that La Llorona might be weeping for *her?*

Josefina swallowed hard. "Try not to worry about La Llorona," she murmured. "How is that tea? Do you think it's helping?"

"Not yet," Doña Felícitas fretted.

Josefina struggled against a wave of frustration. She hadn't been able to help Doña Felícitas. Instead, the old woman had retreated to her bed! Josefina pinched her lips into a tight line, aching to look up and see Teresita coming through the door, or Tía Dolores— or, most especially, Tía Magdalena.

Then Josefina sat up straight. "Why don't you have another sip of tea," she said. "It may take time to work." She held the cup for Doña Felícitas. With her other hand she smoothed the blanket, as if wiping away her thoughts of failure. She *was* going to be a good curandera, and she was *not* ready to admit defeat.

❋

That afternoon, Miguel and Teresita helped Pedro Zamora hobble out to a bench in the courtyard. He wore his sarape, and Josefina could see the outline of the bandage wrapped around his injured leg beneath his trousers.

"Call me when he's ready to go back to bed," Miguel told Teresita.

Teresita and Josefina settled on another bench with a basket of wool to pick free of dirt and bits of straw. "You're looking much better, señor," Josefina said.

"I am better, by God's grace," he said. "And by yours. Your aunt tells me you provided the remedios."

"With Teresita's help," Josefina said. Teresita smiled.

Señor Zamora leaned forward, gazing intently at Josefina. "And I understand you cleaned and mended my clothes."

He suspects that I saw his map, Josefina thought. "Clara did the mending," she told him. "She has more talent with a needle and thread than I do. But sí, I did wash your clothes." Josefina reached for some wool, suddenly needing to keep her hands busy. "Except your sarape. For that, I simply brushed away as much dirt as I could."

"Señorita," Señor Zamora said quietly, "I

must ask. Did you happen to find anything . . .
unexpected as you tended my sarape?"

Josefina darted a glance at him and was
surprised when he suddenly smiled. It was a
warm smile, and it made her *want* to trust him.
She squared her shoulders. "Sí, señor. I did.
I beg your pardon. It fell from your sarape by
accident, and . . ." Her cheeks felt as warm as
midsummer sunshine. "I was curious."

"I understand." Señor Zamora tugged on
his left earlobe absently. "Señorita, I would
like to tell you a story," he began. Then he
glanced toward Teresita.

"I trust Teresita," Josefina said.

"Your story is safe with me," Teresita
agreed, "unless it might bring harm to this
household." Her busy fingers paused.

"No, no." Señor Zamora waved that idea
away like a pesky fly. "Just the opposite, I
hope." He leaned close again. "My tale begins
more than two hundred years ago. Two of my
ancestors were among the first to travel north
from their home in Mexico City into this new

land, *Nuevo México.* One was a priest who sent a letter back to his father in the middle of the 1600s. In that letter he mentions his brother, a soldier."

Josefina nodded. Everyone knew that priests and soldiers were among the earliest Spanish settlers in New Mexico.

"In addition to saving that letter, my family has passed down many tales from those days," Señor Zamora said. "Most of them concern the soldier. He often guarded mule trains transporting gold and silver mined here back to Mexico City, or carrying money intended to pay the men stationed in Santa Fe. His life was often at risk."

"Those were dangerous times," Josefina murmured. She stared at the burr she was working from a lock of fleece, trying to hide her growing excitement.

"Last spring, my father became quite ill. He called me to his bedside and showed me the map you found."

"You'd never seen it before?" Josefina asked.

He shook his head. "Never. That map's existence has been a closely guarded secret." His voice dropped to a whisper. "I believe it's a treasure map!"

Josefina felt that ripple of excitement— the one she'd lost after giving up the search herself—spring back to life. "It does look like it," she agreed.

"I think that the soldier was once forced to hide gold or silver." Señor Zamora waved vaguely toward the front gate and the rocky hills beyond, his gaze distant. "Or perhaps he hid his own savings. Can't you imagine it, señorita? Perhaps he saw bandits stalking one of the payroll caravans. Or perhaps he was escorting settlers south after the Pueblo Revolt, and they realized that they were likely to be attacked."

Josefina had forgotten all about picking wool. "And he never returned for the treasure?"

"The soldier died before he could return to New Mexico, and no one in my family before me took the time to search. But they protected the Zamora family secret, and told no one about the map."

"Señor," Josefina said. "Why are you telling *me* about the secret?"

"Your family saved my life," Señor Zamora said simply. "And if I can find the treasure, I'd like to reward your kindness to a stranger."

Josefina stared at him. "Why—that is very generous!" she said, while her heart sang, *If that happened, I could afford gifts for Francisca and a servant to help Doña Felícitas!*

He shrugged. "It's the right thing to do. I also believe that you and I might be able to help each other, señorita. Surely the treasure is somewhere in the hills near your home. The family legend says the map was made within a day's journey of Santa Fe, but that was all I knew when I left Mexico City last spring. I've been searching for the rock formation shown on the map—"

"Balancing Rock!" Josefina said eagerly.

He smiled. "Is that what you call it? A perfect name. When I saw that formation,

I knew I was in the area where the soldier had buried the treasure. I was so excited, I got careless. That's when I hurt my leg."

Josefina nodded. If she had been in his place, she would have been excited to find Balancing Rock, too! "I understand why your ancestor put a landmark like Balancing Rock on his map," she mused. "But why do you think he picked a turtle and a rainbow?"

"Perhaps he happened to see those things while he was trying to decide where to bury the treasure, and so he chose to use them as symbols," Señor Zamora said. "If he was in immediate danger of attack, he probably didn't think too hard about it."

Josefina imagined herself in such a situation. "It makes me shiver."

"Now that I've finally matched one clue on the map, I *know* I'm getting close." Señor Zamora's eyes sparkled. "But I'm a stranger here. People will become suspicious if I ask questions. Señorita Josefina, I hope that you and I can help each other in this quest."

Josefina's excitement faded, and she ducked her head. "Señor, I must tell you . . . I've already looked for the turtle and rainbow symbols shown on your map," she confessed. "And I asked Miguel, who's walked these hills all his life, if he'd seen them. He said no." She spread her hands, remembering how small she'd felt while studying the endless landscape near Balancing Rock. "Teresita, too."

Teresita gave Josefina a glance that said, *Sí, now I understand some things.*

"The markings might have worn away," Señor Zamora said. "One hundred and forty-six years have passed since the Pueblo Revolt! But I've wondered if the drawing that looks like a rainbow is actually another rock formation. Are there any rock arches nearby?" His expression was hopeful.

Josefina shook her head. "No, señor."

Señor Zamora curled one hand into a fist and lightly pounded it against his good knee. "I have not come so far just to give up my search now."

"You should discuss this with my papá," Josefina said. "He can—"

"No!" Señor Zamora glanced over his shoulder before explaining. "Soon I'll be strong enough to continue my search, and I would like to *find* the treasure before discussing this with anyone else. Someone who knows the landscape better than I might try to find the treasure for himself. And... your papá might think me a fool for even trying to discover the map's secret."

Josefina frowned. "Papá would not do either of those things!" she insisted.

"I'm sure you're right, señorita." His smile returned. "But I hope you'll both keep my secret anyway. Will you do that?"

Teresita nodded. Josefina considered Señor Zamora's request. It *would* be grand to surprise everyone with a successful search! "Sí, señor," she said. "I'll tell no one."

7
TROUBLE BETWEEN SISTERS

That evening, the three sisters gathered
to work on their embroidery. "I love doing
colcha," Clara said with an air of contentment.

Josefina couldn't stop thinking about Señor
Zamora's story, and she made little progress
with her own embroidery. Francisca seemed
distracted, too. "Why do my stitches never
turn out evenly?" she demanded. She dropped
her cloth into her lap.

"It just takes practice," Clara said.

Francisca got up and began to pace. Clara
and Josefina exchanged a troubled glance.
"Francisca, does your head ache again?"
Josefina asked.

Francisca folded her arms over her chest.
"No, but it will if I try to untangle that thread

one more time. I think I'll go make sure the looms are prepared for weaving tomorrow."

"And I'll go check over my supplies in the storeroom," Josefina added quickly. She was too distracted to concentrate on her stitches.

Once in the storeroom, Josefina tried to settle her own nerves. Just as she'd become confident that Señor Zamora was recovering, Francisca had begun complaining of headaches! Would Tía Magdalena return to find half the rancho and village ill?

I must be prepared if Francisca gets another headache, Josefina thought. She stepped from one bundle of drying plants to the next, reviewing what Tía Magdalena had taught her. "Ah!" she murmured when she came across her stash of mallow. As Josefina fingered the broad leaves, Tía Magdalena spoke in her memory: *Headaches can be cured by mashing mallow leaves, adding salt and vinegar, and placing the mixture on the patient's forehead.*

Twilight was descending as Josefina finally stepped from the storeroom. The growing shadows made her thoughts tumble from treasure maps and Francisca's headaches to La Llorona. The first time Josefina had heard the Weeping Woman had been well after full darkness. The second time had been closer to dusk. Would she hear La Llorona tonight? Josefina's mouth grew dry as she glanced at the golondrina holes.

After a moment's consideration, she decided to steal the few minutes of twilight left to listen for the Weeping Woman. She returned to the storeroom and stepped up on the banco beneath the high window. Josefina watched as the evening faded from deep blue to purple. The outbuildings and animal pens stood black against the sky. A coyote howled in the distance. Her tense muscles began to ache.

Then a dog barked, just twice, before abruptly going silent. Josefina caught her breath as the shadowy figure of a woman glided from behind an old cottonwood tree, her long skirts sweeping gracefully as she passed. Josefina strained to make out the woman's appearance, but a rebozo hid her face. In an instant the ghostly figure melted into the night.

Josefina carefully stepped down from her perch and sank onto the banco, giving her pounding heart a moment to slow to its usual beat. Had she just seen La Llorona? Why hadn't she *heard* her this time? Had the rancho's watchdog, trained to confront intruders, stopped barking because it recognized the woman? Or was even the dog frightened by the presence of a ghost?

✳

The next morning, the family gathered after breakfast to bid farewell to Roger Rexford. "God grant you a safe journey," Papá told him.

"Gracias for your help, Señor Montoya," Roger said. He looked at the rancho walls wistfully. "My visit has been even more rewarding than I'd hoped."

"Are you sure you don't wish to stay longer?" Tía Dolores asked.

Roger smiled. "I would like to linger, Señora Romero. But I must return to Santa Fe and see to my work."

Papá inclined his head. "I wish you success, Señor Rexford. If your business ever brings you back to this area, I hope you will honor us with another visit."

"I fully expect my business to bring me back in this direction." Roger gave Papá a calm smile. "I look forward to that visit."

Josefina stood next to Papá as the americano mounted his horse and rode away. "Do you think it's a good idea for Señor Roger and Abuelito to open a saddle shop?" she asked.

"It's difficult for me to form an opinion since I haven't seen any of Señor Rexford's saddles," Papá said. "But your abuelito is a good judge of character and an experienced trader. He wouldn't consider a partnership unless he thought it was promising." He smiled down at Josefina. "There are many changes in the wind, I think."

More than you even know! Josefina thought, thinking of Señor Zamora and the changes that might come if she was able to help him understand his map.

For a moment the two stood silent. Clouds of purple asters bloomed along the road. Streams and irrigation ditches near the rancho's fields glimmered silver in the sun. In the distance, the mountains rose blue-gray against the sky. The hills in between were red and rugged. *I don't know if Señor Zamora and I can find the lost treasure,* she thought. But something about that quiet moment with Papá, looking out over the land they loved, gave her faith.

❄

After Papá went back to work, Josefina went inside and found Señor Zamora slowly limping around the courtyard. Teresita was keeping pace with him, but he walked unaided.

"Señor!" Josefina cried, delighted by his progress. "You're much improved!"

He made a courteous bow. "Sí, señorita."

"You are doing well," Teresita said. "But you must stop before you get overtired."

"My hope gives me strength!" Señor Zamora said. "I feel in my bones that my ancestor's treasure is out there, somewhere, waiting for me to find it. I've located Balancing Rock, so I know I'm getting closer. And now that I'm getting my strength back, I'll soon be able to resume my search." He nodded briskly. "You may both think I'm a foolish man. But I believe I'll find old Santiago Zamora's treasure!"

"Santiago?" Josefina's eyes went wide.

"Sí." Señor Zamora rubbed his chin, looking perplexed. "That was the soldier's given name."

Josefina bounced on her toes. "Señor, the day before you arrived, I found the letter *S* scratched into a rock out in the hills! It was in a sheltered spot, out of the weather. Señor Zamora—your ancestor might have left that mark!"

"It's possible," he said slowly.

Josefina grinned. "Wouldn't his initial make a good mark for the spot where he actually buried the treasure?"

Señor Zamora nodded. "You may have given me the essential clue, señorita! Can you take me to this spot? I don't want to let more time pass! I'm sure I can travel on my horse."

"But... my family is going to the village today to begin preparing for the fiesta honoring San Francisco." Josefina bit her lip. "My papá and Tía Dolores would never understand if I asked to be excused. And besides..."

He smiled. "Preparing is an important part of the celebration."

"Gracias for understanding," Josefina said.

"Perhaps I can show him?" Teresita asked.

Josefina hesitated. She wanted to be there when Señor Zamora dug underneath the *S* and cross! But she couldn't bear to miss a moment of the feast day celebration, even cleaning the church and making decorations. "Sí," she said finally. "You and I have walked near that spot." She described the location.

"I can find it," Teresita said. She looked at Señor Zamora. "Now, señor, you must rest."

"But—"

"The sun has disappeared behind the clouds, and the air is getting colder," Teresita said firmly. "You must gather your strength again before we set out."

Josefina smiled as she watched Señor Zamora walk back inside. He was too determined to rest for long.

❋

"Josefina." Tía Dolores's eyes were troubled when she came looking for her youngest niece that afternoon. "It's time to walk to the village, but Francisca isn't feeling well. She doesn't have a fever, but I haven't been able to suggest anything to bring her comfort." Tía Dolores's fingers drummed lightly against her skirt. "Perhaps you can help."

Josefina hurried to the sleeping sala with worry whispering in her ear. She found Francisca curled on her sheepskin bed beneath a warm woolen blanket.

"Francisca?" Josefina asked, kneeling beside her sister. "Do you have another headache?"

Francisca opened her eyes, then closed them again. "No," she said. "Now my insides feel like they're tied in knots."

"Did you eat anything unusual today?" Josefina asked, struggling to keep her voice low and calm as Tía Magdalena would.

"No!" Francisca curled into a tighter ball.

Josefina rocked back on her heels and drew a deep breath. "Let me make you some cota tea," she began. "It will—"

"I don't want tea!" Francisca flared. "Stop pretending to be a curandera, Josefina. You're just a young girl. You don't know *anything* that can make me feel better. I wish Tía Magdalena were here." She rolled on her side, facing the wall.

Josefina swallowed hard, blinking back sudden tears. She stared at Francisca's back, aching for her sister to look at her, to apologize for saying words that cut into the heart of Josefina's most precious dream. Francisca didn't move. Finally Josefina got stiffly to her feet and left her sister alone.

8

A GHOST IN THE GRAVEYARD

Papá walked Tía Dolores, Clara, and
Josefina to the village in a gloomy drizzle.
Even the cottonwood leaves hung limp and
dull. Josefina plodded silently beside Tía
Dolores. Her heart felt as gray as the clouds.

"My child, I know you're worried about
Francisca," Tía Dolores said. "But she doesn't
have a fever. If Francisca feels better later,
Carmen and Miguel will bring her to the
village."

"I wanted to help her." Josefina's voice
quivered. "But she wouldn't let me."

Tía Dolores took Josefina's hand. "Francisca
has a lot on her mind," she said. "Even the
best remedios won't help a person who needs
something else."

Francisca thinks she needs wealth, so that she can attract the attention of an important family in Santa Fe, Josefina thought wearily. Was Ramón Torres the only person Francisca cared about anymore?

"Do you wish to visit Doña Felícitas today?" Tía Dolores asked.

Josefina did *not* wish to visit Doña Felícitas ... but she had promised that she would. "Sí," she said with a sigh. "For a short while."

When they reached the village, they stopped first at the Aragón home, which was freshly whitewashed and newly scrubbed in honor of the coming celebration. Bunches of goldenrod and purple asters waited on the table. "We brought some red paintbrush plants for the decorations," Tía Dolores told Ofelia's mother.

"Wonderful!" she said. "And I see you brought food as well. Let's take that to the kitchen."

Clara joined the group already making decorations. Josefina carried a basket of *tamales* to the warm kitchen, which smelled spicy-sweet. "Buenas tardes, Soledad!" Josefina said when she saw Ofelia's cousin preparing six round loaves of bread for baking.

Soledad smiled shyly in response. She was using a sharp knife to cut a cross into each loaf. Bowls and platters of food covered the table. Josefina noticed a bowl of what looked like cornmeal mush mixed with berries, and sniffed appreciatively. "This looks interesting!" she said.

Ofelia's mother slid it to the side. "That's not really for the party," she explained. "But we have lots of bizcochitos and other treats."

"Speaking of bizcochitos," Tía Dolores said, "it was kind of you to send that basket home with Josefina."

"I need to say gracias also," Josefina added. "I so appreciated—"

Just then the knife slipped from Soledad's hand and clattered to the floor. Her cheeks flushed.

"No harm done, my child," her aunt said

softly. Soledad and Josefina both stooped to retrieve the knife. As Soledad leaned over, a sturdy wooden cross on a chain slipped out from the neckline of her blouse.

"Oh, Soledad, your cross is beautiful!" Josefina breathed. "May I look at it?" When the older girl nodded shyly, Josefina lifted the cross with her fingers. The wood had been blackened and decorated with tiny bits of golden straw. The intricate design was lovely.

Soledad hesitated, as if considering her words. "My father made it. I turned it into a necklace to keep his memory close."

Josefina gently released the cross. "I can't imagine doing such delicate work."

"It takes practice," Soledad said carefully. "That is . . . my father was quite skilled. I—I'm just starting to practice straw appliqué again. I had to wait until harvest, so I could get clean straw." She tucked the cross back beneath her blouse and rose to her feet.

Ofelia appeared in the doorway. "Josefina, come sit with me! I gathered some yellow

leaves this morning. They'll look beautiful
mixed with these green vines!"

For a moment, Josefina longed to forget
that she had ever dreamed of being a
curandera. She wanted to join the women and
children making decorations for the church.
She wanted to weave flowers into garlands
to honor San Francisco, who had loved plants
and animals just as she did. She wanted to
laugh with Ofelia, and to inhale the dusky
scent of piñón logs burning on the fire, and
to nibble the treats that Soledad brought out
for the workers.

Then she shook her head. "I need to visit
Doña Felícitas first. But I'll be back soon!"

❋

"Do you want me to come inside with
you?" Tía Dolores asked as she and Josefina
approached the widow's door.

Josefina shook her head. "No, gracias. I
promised Tía Magdalena I would do my best
to bring comfort to Doña Felícitas. I haven't

done a very good job so far." She squared her shoulders. "But I'm going to try again."

After the warm glow of Ofelia's home, the widow's dim house felt lonely and cold. Josefina found Doña Felícitas in bed, shivering in spite of her wool blanket. "I'm glad to see you," she said. "I have a chill in my bones."

"It's little wonder!" Josefina said. "Your fire is nearly gone!" She soon had a cheerful fire blazing in the hearth. While waiting for water to boil, she brought in extra wood. She lit the candles in the *araña* hanging from the ceiling and found a second blanket to tuck over Doña Felícitas. "Is that better?" she asked.

"A little." Doña Felícitas gave her a feeble smile.

"We'll try *yerba buena* for your stomach today," Josefina told her. "Hot mint tea." When the water began to bubble, she poured it over the dry mint leaves she'd brought and added a sprinkle of cinnamon and cloves. While the tea was steeping, she gently massaged the widow's aching joints.

Then Josefina helped her sit up in bed and sip the tea. Finally, she sprinkled hot water on some gum weed leaves, piled them on a heated adobe brick, wrapped everything in a thick cloth, and tucked it into bed with Doña Felícitas. "The steam and heat will soothe your bones," Josefina said.

After the dishes had been washed and put away, Josefina looked longingly out the front window toward Ofelia's home. Music spilled from the house and danced through the raindrops: *Come back to your friends! Come back to the fun!*

"Are you feeling better?" she asked, turning to the widow. "My aunt will soon come to fetch me. Everyone has gathered at the Aragóns' home to make decorations."

"And here I am, huddled in bed," Doña Felícitas said sadly. "I loved to make decorations for feast days when I was your age. Now, all I can do is suffer in silence."

Josefina turned away, crossing her arms over her chest as if to hold in the ache of failure. She could see the soft glow of the welcoming lamp hung by the Aragóns' door across the plaza. For the second time that day Josefina felt the sting of unshed tears. *Francisca is right,* she thought. *I have no skills as a curandera. I've tried every remedio I know for Doña Felícitas, and she is as miserable as ever.* She had failed Doña Felícitas, and she had failed Tía Magdalena as well. Thinking back to their last walk into the hills together, Josefina desperately wished that Tía Magdalena were with her.

Then, unexpectedly, she heard in her mind an echo of Tía Magdalena's quiet assurance: *God provides true healers with everything they need—a good memory, a patient and loving heart, and two strong hands.* Josefina closed her eyes and stood very still, letting her aunt's wisdom reach over the miles.

When she finally opened her eyes again, she saw Tía Dolores passing by the window. Josefina quickly opened the door for her aunt. "Are you ready to return to the gathering with me?" Tía Dolores murmured as she pushed her rebozo back from her face.

Josefina shook her head. "No, gracias, Tía Dolores. My teas and salves have not helped Doña Felícitas."

Tía Dolores gently smoothed a strand of hair away from Josefina's face. "I think you've done all anyone could do," she said. "Tía Magdalena would not blame you for returning to the party. You've tried your best."

Josefina managed a smile. "Not quite. I just remembered one more thing to try."

❉

Tía Dolores visited briefly with Doña Felícitas before leaving again. Josefina didn't look at the light shimmering from Ofelia's home as she closed the door firmly behind her aunt. Then she returned to the elderly woman's bedside.

"Doña Felícitas," she said, "may I pray with you?"

The widow's face brightened. "Sí, I would like that."

Josefina knelt and prayed, asking God to
help her bring comfort to Doña Felícitas. Then
Josefina rose and sat by the bed. "You often
mention your childhood," she said. "Will you
tell me some stories from those days?"

A smile blossomed on Doña Felícitas's
wrinkled face. "Why, of course!" She settled
back on her pillows. "As you may know, my
grandparents were among the first to build
a home in this village. My abuelito earned
his living by taking his mule into the hills,
collecting firewood, then bringing it back to
the village to trade or sell. He was poor, but
he had a strong faith and he was content. I
remember sitting on his knee..."

Josefina listened to the old woman's stories
as the afternoon wore toward evening. Tía
Dolores returned with a basket over her arm.
"I brought you some food," she said, handing
Josefina the basket. "Unless you're ready to
leave?" She let the question dangle.

"With your permission, Tía Dolores, I'd
like to stay here until you're ready to return

to our rancho," Josefina said. She knew her family would linger with their friends into the evening. "Please give my apologies to Ofelia and the others."

When Tía Dolores had gone, Josefina sat down by the bed. "See what Tía Dolores brought, Doña Felícitas!" She rummaged in the basket. "Bizcochitos, and some tamales."

Doña Felícitas pushed herself higher on her pillows. "I'll try some bizcochitos," she said. "And another cup of that tea. I'm feeling a little better."

After they'd eaten, Doña Felícitas told more stories about herself as a girl, as a bride, as a wife. Her husband had also earned his living gathering firewood for the villagers. "I often went with him, since God did not give me children to tend," she told Josefina. "Now, as I lie here in bed, I close my eyes and remember the way the hills glowed red at sunset. I remember hearing the larks' tinkling song, and the sweet smell of juniper after a rainstorm."

Josefina felt something sad well in her throat... suddenly followed by something more hopeful. "Doña Felícitas," she began slowly. "You must have come to know the land around the village very well. Do you remember ever seeing a turtle or a rainbow scratched into a rock?" Josefina held her breath. Why hadn't she thought to ask Doña Felícitas this earlier? She was the oldest person in the area.

The elderly woman thought for a long moment, then shook her head. "No, no, I do not recall ever seeing such things."

Josefina tapped her fingers absently on her knee. "How about a rock arch? Have you ever seen a rock formation that looks like a rainbow?"

"Oh, sí, of course."

Josefina could hardly believe what she'd just heard. "*Of course?* Doña Felícitas, I've never seen such a thing!"

Doña Felícitas gave a dismissive wave of her hand. "Rainbow Rock disappeared when I was a child."

Josefina blinked in confusion. "It disappeared?"

"Sí. The arch was once a famous landmark. But it was very thin, very delicate." Doña Felícitas smiled at another memory. "After one fierce rainstorm, the top of the arch crumbled to the earth. I climbed onto one of the fallen rocks and told Abuelito I was standing on top of a rainbow."

"Was Rainbow Rock near Balancing Rock?" Josefina asked eagerly.

"Rainbow Rock was north of Balancing Rock. There was"—she considered—"perhaps the length of three cornfields between them."

"Gracias," Josefina said fervently. "I am most grateful for your help." Her thoughts whirled like autumn leaves in the wind.

Doña Felícitas patted Josefina's hand. "You're a good girl. And your remedios have helped me. I think I'll be able to rest now." She closed her eyes. Josefina hummed a sweet old melody, and soon the widow drifted to sleep.

Josefina tiptoed to the front window. The

light still burned at Ofelia's home, but it was no brighter than the light of satisfaction burning inside of her. She had learned something that might help Señor Zamora. Even better, she'd helped Doña Felícitas. Tía Magdalena had wisely told her the three tools a curandera needed, but for all this time, Josefina had been working with only two: her mind and her hands. When she finally remembered to add a patient heart to her healing arts, she had brought—at long last!— some comfort to the lonely widow.

Josefina smiled. Tomorrow she would offer a special prayer of thanks—

Suddenly all thoughts of the celebration disappeared. The figure of a shawl-draped woman had emerged from the shadows and turned into the churchyard, which was enclosed by a low adobe wall.

Was it someone seeking spiritual comfort? Or was it La Llorona? Josefina stood frozen, torn between dread and her desire to learn who—or what—was slipping ghostlike through the village. Then she pulled her sarape over her head and snatched a spare lantern from the corner. Taking a deep breath, she slipped outside and turned toward the church.

The woman had vanished. Josefina scanned the plaza, the churchyard. All was still. The faint music from the party drifted to her ears, but nothing more.

Just as Josefina was about to scurry back to Doña Felícitas's house, she saw the ghostly woman rise—as if she'd been kneeling by one of the graves in the churchyard. Josefina ran toward the church gate.

Suddenly she stubbed her toe against something hard, lost her balance, and slammed to the ground. "Ay!" she gasped, rubbing one knee. She hadn't seen the ladder that one of the men must have left beside the adobe wall in preparation for attending to repairs. By the time she got back to her feet, the figure was moving quickly through the front gate, a black silhouette against the dark blue-gray dusk.

Josefina tried to follow, but her knee buckled when she put weight on it. The eerie figure melted into the shadows beside the Garcías' home and disappeared. Josefina leaned against the wall. Her breath came quickly, as if she had run a race.

Why did you even try to follow? a voice in her head asked. *What would you have done upon catching La Llorona?*

"I would have tried to bring her some comfort, or peace," Josefina whispered. That's what she wanted to do—although the thought made her insides quiver.

She tested her knee again. It still ached, but it felt strong enough to support her now. She *should* go back to Doña Felícitas's house. It wouldn't do to have Tía Dolores find her outside alone! But after some hesitation, she limped through the churchyard gate instead.

She stared at the church, rising with massive dignity before her. A freshly swept path led from the gate to the church doors. Low grave mounds marked with wooden crosses pressed against the adobe wall on either side of the path. Josefina frowned, trying to remember exactly where the shrouded figure had knelt. None of the graves were very new, for by God's grace, there had been no recent deaths in the village. Whose grave had the woman been visiting?

Josefina stepped carefully to the area where she thought the woman had been. She crouched and lit the candle with trembling fingers, trying to shield the flickering light. She didn't want anyone to see her.

The light illuminated two graves, both so old that the mounds had almost sunk back into the earth. Josefina bit her lip. Could one of these graves possibly be that of La Llorona? Or perhaps the graves of her lost children? Josefina shuddered.

Then something caught her eye. The day's drizzle had softened the earth, and two clear footprints were visible beside her. They were larger than her own, but too small to be a man's.

Josefina sucked in a deep breath and blew it slowly back out. She didn't know much about ghosts, but she was sure they didn't leave footprints. The ghostly figure Josefina had spotted in the churchyard had been alive.

As she crouched in the gloom, thinking that through, Josefina became aware of something else. A plant had grown between the wall and the grave. In her candle's feeble light, the flower heads, shriveled and dry now, glowed a familiar, soft white. Yarrow. Several stalks of the plant had been snapped off. Their roots trailed above ground, as if someone had picked the flowers in haste.

Yarrow was a very useful plant. Prepared in different ways, its leaves and flowers were helpful for soothing burns, easing cold symptoms, and breaking up bad coughs.

And according to some, when plucked from the grave of a young man, yarrow made a potent love charm.

9

Francisca's Surprise

The next morning dawned sunny and clear, but Josefina had trouble sitting quietly through breakfast. "Heavens," Clara whispered as the girls began to clear away plates and platters. "You jiggled through the meal as if you were dancing at a fandango."

"I'm excited about the feast day celebration," Josefina whispered back, although that was only one of the things on her mind. She'd developed a suspicion about the woman she'd seen in the churchyard, and she wanted to pursue it. She was even more anxious to see if Teresita and Señor Zamora had discovered treasure in the hills.

As soon as the morning dishes had been washed, Josefina slipped to the spare sleeping sala and called to Teresita, whom she could hear bustling about inside. "Come in, señorita," Teresita called. "I just brought the señor some tea."

Señor Zamora sat in a chair, pulling on his boots. "How are you this morning?" Josefina asked. "Did you find anything yesterday?"

Señor Zamora sipped his tea. "I'm a little tired," he admitted. "And I'm sorry to say we had no success. Teresita found the S and cross, and I dug beneath them, but I soon hit solid rock. I don't believe those marks you found are very old, anyway." He tugged his earlobe thoughtfully. "Certainly not old enough to have been made by Santiago Zamora."

"Oh." Josefina let herself be disappointed for a moment, then squared her shoulders. "Well, I learned something important yesterday." Quickly she told him and Teresita how Doña Felícitas had described Rainbow Rock.

"Aha!" Excitement brought a sparkle back to Señor Zamora's eyes. He reached for his sarape and pulled the map from its hidden pocket.

Laying it on the table, he traced the line drawn between Balancing Rock and Rainbow Rock. "Perhaps I can find two short rock columns that used to be the ends of the arch."

Josefina stared at the map, wrinkling her forehead. "Perhaps. Still, it will be difficult to find the exact spot where your ancestor buried his treasure."

"Sí." Señor Zamora shrugged. "But we're getting closer!"

Teresita frowned. "I'm worried that you'll re-injure yourself, or become sick again."

"I promise to be careful," Señor Zamora said, but the tone of his voice suggested that fevers, bruises, and aches were of no great concern to him. "I'm preparing to leave the rancho," he told Josefina. "Your papá and your tía have been most generous in their hospitality. I have no wish to overstay my welcome, however. Your news convinces me that it's time I returned to the hills."

"But I wanted you to stay until you discovered Santiago's lost treasure!" Josefina protested. "If you leave now, I'll never know if you find it!"

"You'll know." Señor Zamora's warm grin included both Josefina and Teresita. "By God's grace, my search will soon reach its conclusion. Then I'll return to the rancho and reward you both for your help!"

After Señor Zamora said his farewells to Tía Dolores and Papá, Josefina and Teresita walked him out the front gate, where Miguel had left Señor Zamora's horse. He swung into the saddle with a grimace of discomfort, but gave them a gallant wave with his hat. *"Adiós,* and gracias," he said. "Do not forget your old friend Pedro Zamora!"

Josefina watched as Señor Zamora disappeared down the road. "I was excited about what I learned from Doña Felícitas," she said. "But Señor Zamora might still search for a long time without finding anything." She sighed. "I really thought—or at least hoped—that I could help him solve the puzzle of his map."

"I think it is the quest, with that one,"

Teresita said, fluttering her skirt at a chicken. It squawked and flapped away. "Some men enjoy the hunt itself more than the reward at the end."

Josefina thought about that, staring out toward the distant mountains. She couldn't quite shake her disappointment... but maybe Teresita was right. Señor Zamora had been excited about getting back to work, roaming the hills, searching for clues. Maybe Señor Zamora's true treasure was a life lived out-doors among the red rocks and blue hills, the screeching hawks and the fragrant piñón. "Have fun exploring," she whispered. Then she followed Teresita back inside.

❋

After helping Teresita tidy the spare sala, Josefina walked silently toward the weaving room. Pausing outside, she heard Clara and Francisca bickering about some wool that hadn't come out of a dye pot as golden-hued as they had hoped. *Perfect!* Josefina thought.

That discussion should keep her sisters too busy to wonder why she hadn't come to help.

She hurried back to the sala she shared with Clara and Francisca. After making sure no one was about, she knelt down by the trunk where Francisca kept her belongings and eased open the lid.

Josefina carefully shook out her sister's extra stockings and blouses and skirts. Underneath them she found Francisca's most prized possessions: a strip of lace, her delicate dancing slippers, a string of fancy buttons from the Santa Fe market, a hair comb that had belonged to the girls' mamá. There was nothing else in the trunk.

Josefina sat back on her heels. Had she been wrong? She frowned thoughtfully at her sister's treasures, then picked up one of the thin-soled dancing shoes. When she gently poked one finger into the toe, she felt something odd—

"*Josefina!*"

Josefina whirled to see Francisca in the doorway. "What are you doing?" Francisca demanded angrily. She grabbed the shoe from Josefina's hand. As she did, several things fell to the floor: a scrap of leather, a folded piece of paper, and a tiny bundle of dried yarrow tied with a thread.

Francisca snatched them up. "You have no right to snoop in my things!" she cried.

Josefina swallowed hard. "I couldn't imagine who might be in the churchyard after dark," she said quietly. "Then I found the yarrow plants and remembered Tía Magdalena telling me about the love charm. Later, when I realized that you'd joined everyone in the village after all—"

"I was feeling better." Francisca walked to the doorway and stared out. "But I don't feel well now. So just leave me and my things alone!"

"I might be able to help—"

"You *can't* help!" Francisca said, her voice suddenly more miserable than angry. "You're too young to understand, Josefina. I—I can't stop thinking about someone."

Josefina nodded. "I know. You wanted to make a love charm for Ramón Torres."

"*No!*" Francisca's eyes glittered with tears. "The charm isn't for Ramón Torres! It's for Roger Rexford!"

"Señor *Roger?*" Josefina sat down abruptly on the banco against the wall. "Oh!"

Francisca dropped onto the bench beside her. "I didn't plan for it to happen," she whispered. "I *thought* I knew what I wanted. Ramón is handsome, and dashing, and wealthy . . . but then Roger came. As I watched him getting to know us, I saw what a special person he is. He's funny and kind and adventurous and—and he's just *wonderful!*"

"Does he want to court you?" Josefina asked slowly.

"I think so." Francisca studied her lap as a blush stained her cheeks. "One evening I went to fetch water and sat by the stream— just so I could have a few minutes alone to think. I stayed too long, and as I hurried back up to the rancho, we happened to meet outside. He told me I was the most beautiful girl he'd ever seen."

"Francisca!"

"I told him we couldn't talk there, that it wasn't proper," Francisca said quickly. "I got upset with him, actually. I was afraid someone would see me alone with him, out in the shadows. He said American men didn't have so many rules, and apologized for speaking out of turn. He told me he'd leave something for me in a hole in that old cottonwood tree behind the goat pens. I went back outside the next evening at twilight to fetch it."

It was Francisca talking to Roger that I heard through the golondrina hole that night, Josefina thought. And the woman she'd seen the next evening had been Francisca, hurrying to fetch Roger's note.

Francisca took a deep breath and then unfolded the piece of paper. "It says, '*Para la bella Francisca.*' And he left me this." She extended her palm. A tiny, perfect primrose had been tooled into the scrap of leather.

"Heavens." Josefina didn't know what to think. "I like Roger. But Francisca—he's an americano!" Josefina had never heard of a New Mexican girl marrying an americano.

Francisca folded the letter back into a small square and tucked it away in her dancing shoe with the leather token. "I know."

"And he's not wealthy."

"I *know!*" Francisca said. "But he's someone I could enjoy sharing life with."

Josefina studied her sister. Francisca often changed her mind about things ... but something about her expression told Josefina that this time, she truly knew what she wanted. "Francisca," she said, "if Roger returns, do you think Papá would give him permission to court you?"

Francisca exhaled slowly. "I don't know."

"I think you should talk with Tía Dolores," Josefina told her.

"I can't talk with Tía Dolores!" Francisca protested. "It—it's scandalous to discuss such a thing! Roger must decide if he wants to approach Papá."

"But this is an unusual situation," Josefina insisted. "If Roger does come back, it might help if Tía Dolores, at least, had some warning."

"I couldn't talk to Tía Dolores about Roger," Francisca moaned. "I just couldn't. But— would you talk to her for me?"

"Why *me?*"

Francisca rubbed her forehead. "Oh, I'm getting another headache. Please, Josefina? Would you talk to her for me?"

Josefina turned away from the pleading look in her sister's eyes. The idea of carrying Francisca's hopes on her shoulders made Josefina nervous. But Francisca's anxiety about Roger was making her sick! One way or another, Francisca needed to know what Tía Dolores and Papá might think.

"Sí," Josefina agreed reluctantly. "I don't know what I'll learn. But I think that whatever Tía Dolores says will be more useful to you than a charm of dried yarrow."

"I know." Francisca smiled. "Gracias. And Josefina . . . I'm sorry I was so mean to you. You'll be a wonderful curandera one day, I know it."

Francisca's compliment made a primrose of happiness bloom in Josefina's heart. Then a sudden question pinched the back of her mind. "But why were you outside crying the very night Señor Roger arrived at the rancho? Were you thinking then of Ramón Torres?"

Francisca stared at her, nose wrinkled in confusion. "What are you talking about?"

"But if it wasn't you, then . . ." Josefina felt her bones grow cold again. Then who? She had heard a weeping woman outside the rancho that night, and several of the villagers had heard her, too.

Was some other woman defying strict custom and wandering alone at night? Or was La Llorona, with her weeping and wailing and omens of death, still roaming after all?

10

THE WIDOW'S TRUNK

"You are quiet today, señorita," Teresita observed later that morning, as she and Josefina walked to the village. "The weather is fine, and tomorrow is San Francisco's feast day. This should be a happy time!"

Suddenly, Josefina didn't want to keep her fears locked inside for another moment. "I heard a woman weeping outside the rancho a few days ago," she said. "Since then, several villagers have heard her. People say that hearing La Llorona is an omen of death."

"Do you believe that, señorita?" Teresita asked.

"At first I was afraid it might be true," Josefina confessed. "Then Señor Zamora got better, and Doña Felícitas is a little better too.

But La Llorona still troubles me." Josefina kicked at a rock in the road. "I think that just worrying about the Weeping Woman can make people sick."

They had reached the village. Smoke plumed from a dozen chimneys. Señora López was sweeping her front step but stopped to call a greeting. Señor Sánchez sat on a bench in the sun, whittling, and several small boys dashed back and forth in a noisy game. Josefina felt a sweet ache in her heart. She didn't want any trouble to darken this village.

If I can learn something about the Weeping Woman, Josefina told herself, *I might be able to calm my friends' fears.* La Llorona had recently been heard only near the village, and Josefina was usually at the rancho when darkness fell. But her family would return to the village that very evening when the men built bonfires near the church to herald the eve of San Francisco's feast day. *I must watch for La Llorona tonight,* Josefina thought. The idea made her shiver, for she didn't know if her neighbors were mistaking a living woman for La Llorona, or if they truly were hearing the sobs of a long-dead mother grieving for her children. But she knew she had to try.

"You're right to worry, señorita," Teresita said softly. "Fear is a powerful thing."

The servant stared at the distant hills as if seeing another time, another place. Josefina could tell that Teresita was thinking of more than La Llorona. "It must have been very frightening to be taken captive by your enemies, and to be stolen from your own people," Josefina said, choosing her words carefully. They had never spoken of this before.

"Sí," Teresita said. "It was."

"Did you ever try to run away?" Josefina asked. She couldn't imagine what would have been more frightening—being stolen from her family, or trying to escape from her captors and make her way home through a strange land, all alone.

"I looked for a chance to run away," Teresita

said. "But as time passed, I realized it might be difficult to return to my own people. The experience—living with people so different from you—it changes who you are."

Josefina put a hand on Teresita's arm. "I'm sorry that happened to you," she said. "But I'm glad you came to live with us, Teresita."

"Sí, I am too." Teresita smiled, and her eyes lost their faraway look. "Come along, señorita. Doña Felícitas will be glad to see you."

❋

"How nice that Señora García brought you this lovely stew today," Josefina said to Doña Felícitas a short while later as she stirred the kettle she'd hung over the fire.

"Sí, but she also brought more tales of La Llorona wandering about the village at night." Doña Felícitas shook her head sadly.

"Will you tell me more stories about the old days?" Josefina asked. She wanted to help Doña Felícitas forget about La Llorona for a while.

Doña Felícitas's weathered face crinkled into a smile—perhaps the first genuine, come-from-the-inside smile Josefina had ever seen from the widow. "In a moment," the old woman said. "Por favor, go to that trunk there by the front window. Open it."

Surprised, Josefina obeyed. She found an odd assortment of things neatly packed inside the old trunk—a rusted spur, a broken piece of Pueblo pottery, the sole of an old shoe. She couldn't decide if she was looking at prized possessions or old rubbish.

"Look for a round piece of blue-and-white pottery," Doña Felícitas called from the bed.

"I have it." Josefina pulled out a whorl of pottery, slightly larger than her palm. A smooth stick extended from a hole in the middle of the disk. She brought it to the widow. "It looks like a spindle for spinning wool, but I've never seen one made of pottery before."

"My abuelito made this *malacate*," Doña Felícitas told her. "He found some pottery one day in the hills. A traveler had broken a plate, I imagine, and tossed the pieces aside. So my abuelito shaped one of the pieces to fit a spindle." She pressed it back into Josefina's hands. "You have been very kind to an old woman. I know you missed the party yesterday, just to keep me company. I'd like you to have it."

"Oh . . . *gracias!*" Josefina twirled the spindle, delighted by the play of color. "Your abuelito must have been a clever man."

"He was." Doña Felícitas settled back against her pillows. "He found all sorts of things up in the hills over the years. And he met many people. Travelers. Bandits hiding in the hills—those he stayed away from. Shepherds. Treasure seekers—"

"Your abuelito met someone searching for lost treasure?" Josefina leaned closer, questions dancing on the tip of her tongue.

"Sí, one time. At least we think so." The widow stared at the ceiling. "My abuelito once found a stranger out in the hills the day after a terrible storm had blown through. The man

135

was soaked and shivering. All of his food had been ruined."

"Had he been searching for treasure?"

Doña Felícitas smiled, wanting to tell the story her own way. "My abuelito brought the man home. We got him warm and dry and full of good food. He stayed with us for a week. The last night, he took a piece of paper out of a little leather pouch he carried and spread it out—right there on that table." She pointed to the table where Josefina had often prepared food or remedios.

"Was it a treasure map?" Josefina asked eagerly.

"No! More like instructions, but they didn't make sense. And there were two pictures among the words, also." Doña Felícitas nodded thoughtfully, remembering. "The traveler said he'd found the paper among his papá's things after he died. The traveler believed that his papá had marked those symbols out in our hills years earlier. Our guest had tried to find them, but he told my abuelito that he was tired of chasing legends. In thanks for the shelter he received here, he gave the paper to my abuelito. 'May it bring you more luck than it brought me,' the man said."

"Doña Felícitas," Josefina said, struggling to keep her voice even. "Do you remember what the pictures on the paper looked like?"

"Of course!" The widow looked delighted at Josefina's interest. "But why don't you see for yourself? The paper is in the trunk with the rest of my abuelito's things."

Josefina darted to the trunk, knelt beside it, and began carefully removing items and laying them aside—a gourd canteen, a battered hat, a smooth red and tan stone. "Look for the pouch," Doña Felícitas called. "The paper is still in the pouch."

"I found it." Josefina pulled out a large, weather-stained leather pouch. She tugged on the drawstring, which was stiff with disuse. Inside the pouch was a folded piece of paper. Josefina's fingers trembled as she gently pulled it free. She returned to her seat beside

the bed before easing open the ancient folds.
Three sides of the paper were cut straight.
The right side was ragged, as if this piece had
come from a larger piece of paper that had
been torn in two.

"See?" Doña Felícitas asked. "Most of it is
writing."

Josefina squinted at the faded ink. "You're
right," she said. "These instructions don't make
much sense. At least not by themselves." Her
heart began to beat too fast. "Doña Felícitas,
I think this is only *half* of a treasure map."

"Half? Well . . . that could be." The old
woman tapped the paper lightly with a thin
finger. "What of those symbols, though? My
abuelito never saw a coiled snake marked into
a rock, and neither did I. Have you ever seen
such a mark?"

"No," Josefina said. "But I know who has!"

11
SEARCHING FOR GOLD

"Señor Zamora!" Miguel called. "Señor Zamora, where are you?" His cries echoed among the rocky hills. The only reply was the wild *"keeer"* of a red-tailed hawk circling high above them.

"The señor can't be too far from here," Josefina said. They were walking north from Balancing Rock. "He was going to search for whatever might be left of Rainbow Rock."

Teresita smiled at her. "Don't worry, señorita. We'll find him."

I hope it's soon! Josefina thought, shading her eyes with her hand as she searched the horizon. Although only hours had passed since Doña Felícitas had given Josefina permission to borrow the old paper, it felt as if months had crawled by.

Miguel called again. "Señor Zamora!"
This time, an answering shout bounced back
to them. Josefina grinned with relief as Señor
Zamora appeared from around a thicket of
scrubby oaks and grass, leading his horse.

"Señorita Josefina!" he said, looking
surprised. "And Miguel, and Teresita! I didn't
expect to see you so soon."

"Señor, por favor," Josefina cried, "will you
get out your map? It's important!"

Looking perplexed, Señor Zamora reached
under his sarape and retrieved his map. He
spotted a flat rock nearby, which he used as
a table. As Señor Zamora carefully unfolded
his precious map, Josefina retrieved Doña
Felícitas's paper from its pouch and did the
same. Everyone crowded close as she gently
placed her paper beside Señor Zamora's.

The two fit together perfectly.

"*Señorita!*" Señor Zamora breathed. "Where
did you get that?"

"From a friend," Josefina said. She quickly

told him the story. "I didn't think you'd mind if I confided in Doña Felícitas and Miguel."

"Not at all." Señor Zamora sounded dazed.

Miguel scratched his head. "So, are we looking for *two* treasures?"

"I don't think so," Josefina said. As she studied the pieces of paper side by side, she began bouncing with excitement. "I think we had it all wrong, Señor Zamora! We assumed that your paper was a map. It was designed to *look* like a map. But I think it's really a key, or a legend. Just look—when we line up the instructions with the symbols, we get a very different set of directions."

"You're right!" Señor Zamora said. "The first line on your paper reads, *Begin at this rock formation just after sunrise.* That instruction is written directly across from the drawing of Rainbow Rock on my paper." He pointed.

Josefina continued to read. "*Stand in the farthest curve of its shadow with your right shoulder facing*"—her finger dropped down a space on the paper before she could finish the sentence—"*this formation.*" Her finger then lightly traced a line to the sketch of Balancing Rock.

"My half of the map makes it seem that one must walk from Rainbow Rock toward Balancing Rock." Señor Zamora's voice was rising. "Instead, Balancing Rock is used only as a reference. We should be walking *away* from it instead."

Josefina nodded. "Exactly!"

"This new piece of the map surely came from a friend or comrade of Santiago's," Señor Zamora said. "Perhaps Santiago and another soldier buried the treasure together. They might have decided to tear the map in two and then travel separately. If one of the men were captured by bandits, the thieves wouldn't be able to easily locate the treasure."

Miguel squinted at the paper. "Santiago and his comrade were very clever. But what does the map say next?"

"The instructions say to go in the *opposite* direction of the two feathered arrows,"

Josefina told him, including Teresita in her explanation.

Señor Zamora's dirty finger hovered over the map. "Here on the new piece is a sketch of another turtle, and the directions say to *Follow as directed.* That instruction is repeated below, opposite the turtle drawn on my map."

"I think Santiago meant that we should walk in the direction the turtles are facing," Josefina said.

"Look here, though," Señor Zamora said. "The very last instruction, right by this drawing of a coiled snake on the new piece, says *Dig here.*" He pulled off his hat and ran a hand through his hair. "But we haven't discovered any of Santiago's original marks in the rocks! This is a wonderful find, señorita, but I don't think we're any closer to locating the treasure!"

"All we need is that coiled snake." Josefina beamed. "And Miguel knows where to look."

❋

For the next hour or so, Miguel led the others back and forth through a stretch of rocky hills about a mile from Balancing Rock. Sometimes he paused, scratching his chin as he squinted at the landscape. Other times, when some landmark clicked in his memory, he stepped forward with confidence. Señor Zamora twitched with impatience, but he managed to hold his tongue.

Finally Miguel stopped, staring up a stony wash below a cliff. His eyes narrowed, and he nodded slowly. "I think it's this way," he said. "I remember looking for a stray lamb up there."

Señor Zamora led the scramble up the slope. "It's here!" he yelled. He pointed to the image of a coiled snake scratched into a large rock that was sheltered by a ceiling of stone jutting from the cliff wall. As he hastily retrieved his shovel from the bundle tied behind his saddle, Josefina crouched by the picture.

These marks were made before Doña Felícitas's abuelito was born! she thought with wonder, touching the faint image. In her mind she could see Santiago Zamora crouching in this very spot, using a knife or a sharp rock to etch the image of a coiled snake into the stone.

Señor Zamora's shovel rasped into the soil. "We must dig carefully," he said, grunting as he tossed aside the first bit of dirt. "We don't want to damage the treasure." He dug until he was winded, and then Miguel took a turn. Teresita and Josefina stood to the side, watching every move.

Finally, when Miguel was panting for breath, Señor Zamora took up the shovel again. On his very next scoop the blade made a new sound, a dull *thunk.* "There's something here!" he cried. "We've found it!" Dropping to his knees, he began scooping away dirt and gravel with his hands. Miguel quickly knelt to help. Josefina clasped her hands together as a dark, flat shape emerged. The two men slowly uncovered a large, rectangular wooden box.

Señor Zamora rocked back on his heels. "This trunk is as long as you are tall, señorita!

I had imagined a jar of gold coins, or perhaps a small box . . . nothing like this." He wiped a trickle of sweat from his forehead with one arm.

"Let's lift the box out," Miguel suggested. "Careful! The wood is so old that it's starting to crumble." He wriggled his hands under one end of the box, and Señor Zamora followed his example on the other end. With a final tug, they pulled the box free from the hole and placed it on the ground.

Señor Zamora brushed dirt and loose gravel from the box with a gentle hand. "Santiago, my ancestor, was the last man to touch this," he said with awe. "Before I uncover the treasure, I want to say that I believe God led me to the Montoya rancho for a reason. Without your help, I would never have found the treasure. Whatever is inside this box, however great the wealth, I will share it with *all* of you."

The box lid had been nailed into place, so Señor Zamora fetched a chisel from his pack and began to pry the lid free. With each thrust the wood groaned a little, but the ancient nails gave way, one by one. Josefina nibbled her lower lip, noticing shadows lengthening along the ground. Her family would soon begin to wonder why she and Teresita and Miguel had not returned, and she didn't want them to worry. *Hurry, Señor Zamora!* she urged silently. *Hurry!*

Finally Señor Zamora worked his way around the box. He nodded at Miguel, and the two men lifted away the wooden lid. Teresita and Josefina stepped closer, peering to see. The treasure was wrapped in heavy canvas. Señor Zamora wiped his hands on his trousers—which were no cleaner than he was—before grasping the top edge of the old canvas and pulling it aside.

Josefina saw a glint of gold just as she heard Señor Zamora's shocked exclamation. For a long moment, no one seemed able to find words.

12

SECRETS REVEALED

That evening, as the village men began to place wood near the church for their bonfires, Tía Dolores accompanied Josefina and Señor Zamora to Doña Felícitas's house. "Buenas tardes," Josefina called from the doorway. "May we come in?"

"Of course!" Doña Felícitas beckoned them inside. Josefina was delighted to see that the elderly woman had ventured from her bed to the chair beside the fireplace. "Is this the man you were telling me about this morning?" Doña Felícitas asked.

Josefina introduced Señor Zamora. He carefully eased his canvas-wrapped bundle down on the widow's table, then snatched his hat from his head and bowed. "I owe you a great debt," he said. "Without your paper, we never would have found my ancestor's treasure."

Doña Felícitas's face crinkled into a smile. "My abuelito would be pleased to know that the paper he saved all those years finally served its purpose! What did you find?"

"A surprise." Señor Zamora reverently pulled the canvas away to reveal a golden cross. Even in the dim light, it sparkled as he held it up for the widow to see.

"Oh!" Doña Felícitas gasped, her eyes filling with tears. "It's beautiful!"

Tía Dolores smiled. "Why don't you tell her the story, Josefina?"

"We think this is the cross you told me about," Josefina said. "The one that used to hang in our church years ago. You thought the priest took it along when he and the villagers fled south during the Pueblo Revolt. Instead, he buried it out in the hills for safekeeping."

Señor Zamora picked up the story. "A map has been handed down in my family,

as Señorita Josefina told you this morning.
I always believed that it had been made by
my ancestor Santiago Zamora, a soldier." He
looked at Josefina.

"When I saw that the paper Doña Felícitas
owned was covered with writing, I started
to wonder," Josefina said. "I didn't know
whether the soldier knew how to read and
write. But I knew that his brother, the priest,
did. Señor Zamora had told me that the
only letter his family has from that time was
written by the priest, not the soldier."

Señor Zamora returned the cross to the
table. "He and another man must have
worked together to hide the cross safely. For
whatever reason, neither of them was ever
able to return it to the church."

"I thank God for this day," Doña Felícitas
said. "Josefina, when you told me your tale
of lost treasure this morning, I never imagined
you'd find this!"

"I'm the most surprised of all!" Señor
Zamora said with a rueful chuckle. "Well, I

have always been a poor man, and it's not such a bad thing. This cross belongs to your church."

"We've already shown it to Padre Simón," Josefina told Doña Felícitas. "He's going to hang it in the church—just in time for San Francisco's feast day! But he agreed to let us bring it here to show you."

"Gracias, my child." Doña Felícitas reached for Josefina's hand and pressed it between her own. "You've made me very happy."

❇

A short while later, Josefina's family and Señor Zamora joined the hushed line of villagers filing toward the church on a path marked by brilliant bonfires. Josefina felt a lump rise in her throat as she entered the church. The walls shone with a fresh coat of whitewash. Candles glowed softly from the altar. The embroidered altar cloth was freshly laundered and ironed. The statue of San Francisco showed a smile that seemed too sweet to be carved from wood. And on the wall behind the altar, the golden cross shone with a glory Josefina could only imagine came straight from heaven. Padre Simón would celebrate Mass in the morning, but for now, everyone was content to sit in reverent silence.

Later, as they stepped back outside, Josefina leaned toward Señor Zamora and whispered, "I hope you aren't too disappointed that you didn't find gold or silver coins."

Señor Zamora tugged his ear as he considered. "I truly am a rastreador," he said. "I'll go back to my job, seeking lost animals for wealthy ranchers. It allows me to do what I love best—roam about under the open sky. I had promised a reward to you and Teresita and Miguel, though. And now I have nothing to share. For that, I'm sorry."

"I remember you saying that you wanted to share the treasure with all of us," Josefina told him. She waved a hand, indicating her friends and neighbors. "And you did. Returning the cross is worth more to us than you could have imagined."

Some of the women brought platters of food out to the plaza. Ofelia Aragón squeezed through the crowd to stand by Josefina. "Tell me everything!" she whispered in Josefina's ear. "People are saying that *you* helped bring our cross back from the hills!"

"I'll let Señor Zamora tell the story," Josefina whispered back, stifling a happy giggle. "Look—everyone wants to hear him."

Señor Zamora proved to be a natural storyteller. He described his hot, dusty, sometimes hungry search. He told of his excitement upon recognizing Balancing Rock, of injuring himself, of his illness. "After regaining some of my strength," he continued, "I still followed false leads. Señorita Josefina told me of finding a letter *S* scratched into a rock."

"Oh!" someone near Josefina gasped.

Ofelia turned to her mother. "Mamá?" she whispered. "Are you all right?"

"Sí, sí." Her mother waved a dismissive hand. "Someone stepped on my toes."

"I had no choice but to investigate," Señor

Zamora was saying. "I dug until my back ached, but there was nothing to find. My hopes were dashed again."

The listeners sighed in sympathy. Josefina, though, stopped listening. Despite all the excitement of finding the cross, she hadn't forgotten the challenge she had set for herself: to watch and listen for La Llorona.

Josefina looked thoughtfully at Ofelia's mother. She seemed to be scanning the crowd. Then her shoulders slumped, as if in sadness—as if she hadn't seen who or what she was looking for.

Josefina thought back over the days since La Llorona had first been heard. She considered odd moments that had almost escaped notice at the time but that, when studied together, made a new idea take shape in her mind.

"I'll be back soon," she whispered to Ofelia. She slipped to the edge of the crowd, where she could better look from face to face in the flickering shadows. One face was missing.

Josefina slid through the crowd to join

Francisca. Earlier, Josefina had asked Tía
Dolores whether it would be possible for an
americano to court a New Mexican girl. During
the walk to the village that day, she'd told
Francisca their aunt's response, given after a
moment of silence: "It might be." Then Josefina
had told Francisca about hearing La Llorona
and asked for her help.

"It's time," Josefina told Francisca now.
It wasn't proper for young girls to roam about
at night without a chaperone, but Josefina
didn't see any other way to follow her hunch.
At least she and Francisca would be together.

The two girls pulled their rebozos over
their heads and slipped away from the crowd,
into the shadows. Señor Zamora had finished
his story. Someone brought out a violin, and
its sweet tune slid through the night. Josefina
knew that people would linger for a while, but
the *real* celebration would follow tomorrow's
Mass. Right now, she didn't have much time.

"Josefina, where are we going?" Francisca
hissed.

"I have an idea." Josefina thought they should try looking—and listening—behind the Aragón home first. After reaching the house, she pulled Francisca into the deep shadows between the Aragóns' home and their neighbors'.

They emerged behind the houses, beside the Aragóns' moonlit garden. Francisca jerked Josefina's sleeve and gave her a sister-look that said, *What are we doing here? This doesn't make sense, and I want to go back and join the others.* Josefina frowned in return: *Not yet.* She didn't like being here, either. The house hid the bonfires from sight. The open terrain beyond the village seemed to stretch forever into the darkness. But she wasn't ready to give up. She forced her feet to walk farther from the house.

Suddenly she froze. Francisca squeezed her hand so hard that it hurt. They had both heard the sound—a faint sob. "La Llorona?" Francisca gasped.

"I don't think so." Josefina took a deep

breath. A small open shelter roofed with branches stood behind the garden, and she thought the weeping came from that *ramada*. She tiptoed toward the sound, towing Francisca along. As they reached the ramada, Josefina saw the silhouette of a young woman sitting on a bench. "Soledad?" Josefina called softly. "It's Josefina Montoya and my sister Francisca."

Soledad quickly swiped at her cheeks with her hands. "Wh–what do you want?" she asked.

"Just to talk," Josefina said as she and Francisca stepped inside and sat down across from her. "Sometimes it helps to talk about a problem."

Soledad blew her nose. "I don't have any problems," she said in that slow, measured tone Josefina had noticed before.

Josefina bent her head. Why had she thought she should confront Ofelia's cousin herself? She should have talked with Tía Dolores, or waited until Tía Magdalena returned. They would have known what to do.

Francisca touched Josefina's arm. "Come along," she said quietly. "I think Soledad wants to be alone."

Josefina gathered her skirts but couldn't bring herself to rise without making one more attempt. "Soledad," she said gently, "how long were you a cautiva?"

Soledad gasped. Her mouth moved, but no words emerged. Finally she stammered, "H–how did you know?"

"I didn't know," Josefina admitted. "Not until just now. I should have guessed earlier, though. *You* tucked that string of Navajo tea bundles into the basket of bizcochitos, didn't you? Just as I was about to thank your aunt for it, on the day everyone gathered to make decorations, you dropped the knife."

"I heard you worrying about Doña Felícitas," Soledad murmured. "I wanted to help."

"That same day, I saw a bowl filled with food I didn't recognize," Josefina added. "Was it a Navajo dish?"

Soledad began rubbing her arms as if she

were cold. "One of my favorites—sumac berries cooked with cornmeal."

"You gathered the sumac berries near our rancho," Josefina guessed. "I found a beautiful hair tie caught in a sumac bush, near an alder tree where someone had been gathering bark. Our Navajo servant Teresita is the only other person I know who uses such ties."

A burst of laughter drifted from the plaza. Soledad looked out at the night. "I was stolen from my family by Navajo raiders when I was fourteen, and taken in by a Navajo family who had lost a daughter of their own."

Josefina felt a painful twist in her heart.

"Did you escape from the Navajo?" Francisca asked softly. "Or were you traded?"

"I stayed with the Navajo for several years. I had no idea how to get home! But one day another captured New Mexican arrived. He was a boy, just twelve or so, but he told me he knew how to get back to the nearest town. He was determined to run away, and when the time came, I—I ran with him."

"And you made it safely." Josefina tried to imagine what that journey had been like.

"It was very hard, but... sí, we made the journey safely." Soledad's voice was dull. "By the time I returned home, though, my parents had died." She wiped away a tear that trickled down her cheek.

Francisca moved to the other bench and put an arm around Soledad's shoulders. "We're so sorry," she whispered. "Our mamá died three years ago, so we understand—at least a tiny bit."

"I came here to live with my mother's sister and her family." Soledad tried to smile. "My aunt had prayed for my return. She was so upset when her prayers weren't answered that she took the statue of San Antonio from her family altar and hid it in the hills."

"Did she mark the spot with an *S* and cross?" Josefina asked. "She seemed startled when someone mentioned the *S* tonight. That's what helped me start putting all the clues together."

Soledad nodded. "We went and fetched

the statue together, after I arrived here. My aunt loves me ... but she worries, too. She said that people here would feel uncomfortable if I spoke about my time with the Navajos."

"It must be difficult to keep that secret," Francisca murmured.

"Sometimes I start to talk and a Navajo word comes out," Soledad said. "I have to think about what I'm going to say before I say it. The Navajo way of speaking is different from Spanish. Navajos often describe things instead of giving them a name."

That explains Soledad's hesitant speech, Josefina thought.

Soledad finally looked up. "Sometimes the secret of my time as a cautiva grows inside me until I feel ready to burst!" she exclaimed. "For a long while I held my sadness and loneliness inside. But when autumn came ... My papá's favorite season was autumn, you see. I miss him so much."

"It's terrible to lose someone you love," Josefina whispered. "I remember how hard

I cried when our mamá died. It was you
I heard weeping near our rancho last week,
wasn't it?"

Soledad pulled the cross she wore around
her neck from beneath her blouse, stroking
it lightly. "Every fall Papá and I would walk
together to nearby ranchos to collect the fresh
straw he used to decorate his wooden crosses
and boxes. One night I wandered down the
road toward your rancho."

"All by yourself?" Josefina couldn't help
asking.

Soledad shrugged. "That must shock you.
But after all of my experiences . . . it's hard to
worry so much about such things. Anyway,
I needed to be alone. It was the first time I felt
free to cry, since I didn't think anyone would
hear me. I saw the alder bark and remembered
my Navajo mother using it to dye wool. I
found the sumac berries, and I couldn't resist
picking some. Then I saw the beautiful wheat
waiting to be threshed outside your rancho.
I hope you don't mind, but I took a little so

I could practice my own straw appliqué."

"We don't mind at all," Josefina said quickly. "Your papá would be proud to know you're continuing his work."

"That's a nice thought." Soledad tucked the cross away. "You should go back now, before someone comes looking for you."

Josefina knew Soledad was right. Still, she could tell that their visit had done little to ease Soledad's sadness. "How can we help you?" she asked.

"You can't," Soledad said. "The truth is . . . I don't know where I belong anymore. My aunt loves me, but she's uncomfortable with me sometimes. I've even thought about going back to the Navajo. They were kind to me, but I don't belong there, either. No one can ever really understand."

"That may be true," Francisca agreed slowly. "But I hope we can be friends. Won't you come back to the plaza with us?"

"Please?" Josefina added. She couldn't bear to leave Soledad alone.

Soledad hesitated, then sighed. "All right," she said.

The three of them walked back around the house in silence. In the plaza, groups of people still clustered by the bonfires—talking, laughing, listening to the music. No one had missed them. But Josefina still wanted to do *something* more to help Soledad.

Suddenly she had an idea. "Wait," she said. She leaned toward Francisca and whispered in her ear. Francisca listened intently, then nodded and slipped away. Soledad didn't move. Telling her tale seemed to have exhausted her.

Josefina watched as Francisca made her way to a small group of servants on the edge of the gathering. Francisca took Teresita aside and spoke urgently for a moment. Then the two walked back to Josefina and Soledad.

Teresita put a gentle hand on Soledad's arm. *"Yá'át'ééh,"* she said, greeting Soledad in Navajo. "I understand we have much in common."

13
HEART'S DESIRE

The next day, Josefina's heart ached with joy as one of the local men reverently carried the cross from the church. The treasure glowed golden in the morning sun as he began the procession through the village. Several women followed, holding a beautiful banner painted with an image of San Francisco. The villagers walked in two lines—men and boys on one side, women and girls on the other. Another man carried the statue of San Francisco, and Padre Simón followed at the rear.

Josefina walked proudly, dressed in her finest clothes. She caught her breath as the procession neared Doña Felícitas's house on their way back to the church. The widow stood in her doorway, supported by Soledad.

After Mass was over, everyone poured back outside the church. Josefina found Doña Felícitas and Soledad sitting on a sunny bench in front of the widow's house. "Doña Felícitas!" she exclaimed. "I didn't expect to see you outside!"

"Your remedios must be working," Doña Felícitas said. "And Señorita Soledad came to help me this morning." She sighed with contentment. "It was a joy to watch the procession."

"Will you be all right for a few moments?" Soledad asked Doña Felícitas. "I wish to speak to Josefina."

"Oh sí, sí. You girls go on." Doña Felícitas waved a hand. "I can see everything from here. Perhaps you will be so kind as to bring me some of that good food."

"I wanted to say gracias, Josefina," Soledad said as they walked toward the big tables the men had set up in the plaza.

Josefina smiled. "I did very little."

"It was your idea to fetch Teresita," Soledad

reminded her. "Talking with her made me feel better. She truly understands."

"I'm so glad." Josefina squeezed her hand.

"And Teresita suggested that I help Doña Felícitas," Soledad added. The girls stopped, waiting politely as the adults began filling their plates with tortillas and tamales, chicken with rice, bizcochitos and custard. "She needs a companion, and I need to feel useful."

Josefina smiled again, remembering her wish to hire a servant for Doña Felícitas. This solution was much better.

Ofelia joined them then, with Clara and Francisca close behind. Everyone feasted until they couldn't eat another bite. Then several men brought out guitars and violins. On this most joyous of all days, dancing and games would last for hours.

Josefina was sitting with her family when a man on horseback trotted into the plaza, accompanied by another man driving a wagon. Josefina squinted at the wagon, then clapped her hands. "It's Abuelito! And Tía Magdalena!"

"And *Roger!*" Francisca breathed, staring at the rider.

"Buenas tardes les dé Dios," Abuelito said, his eyes sparkling with the fun of surprising everyone.

Papá greeted his sister and father-in-law warmly, then turned to their companion. "Señor Rexford! I didn't expect to see you again so soon."

Roger had waited politely since dismounting, but now he stepped square in front of Papá. "Buenas tardes, Señor Montoya. As I said when we parted, I have business here."

"Oh?" Papá looked confused, but Josefina noticed Tía Dolores glancing from Roger to Francisca with eyes narrowed thoughtfully.

Roger pulled his horse forward. Josefina gasped as she got her first good look at the saddle on the horse's back. Her fingers longed to trace the intricate patterns tooled into the leather, to touch the sparkling silver adornments, to flutter the decorative leather tassels.

Papá stepped closer. "Did you make this

fine saddle, Señor Rexford?"

"I did," Roger answered. "It was the last saddle I made before leaving Missouri. I've kept it packed away with my baggage ever since. I brought it out to show Señor Romero, who's decided to go into business with me." He glanced at Abuelito, who nodded, and then back at Papá. "But I also needed to show it to you, Señor Montoya. I am a good craftsman. I can earn a comfortable living."

Francisca grabbed Josefina's hand.

"I can see that's true," Papá said cautiously. "But my father-in-law, as your business partner, is the only one who must be assured of that."

"I came here today to discuss another partnership," Roger said. "Señor Montoya, may I have your permission to court Francisca?"

Francisca squeezed Josefina's hand *hard*. From behind the family group came the joyous strains of music. Papá stared silently at Roger, his face expressionless. Josefina held her breath.

"This question requires some thought,"

Papá finally said. "You're an americano, and that..." His voice trailed away.

"Sí, I am an americano," Roger said. "But I have come to truly appreciate this beautiful land and its people."

"What about your dream of returning to Missouri?" Tía Dolores asked. "What about your—how do you say it—maple tree?"

"I have a better dream now," Roger said, spreading his palms as if discarding those old ideas then and there. "One that will keep me right here in New Mexico. Going into business with Señor Romero is only the first step."

Papá looked at Tía Dolores. Josefina thought she saw her aunt give Papá a tiny nod, as if to say, *I know this is a surprise, but perhaps you should not say no right away. Get to know this young man better. Perhaps his idea has merit.*

Finally Papá turned back to Roger. "We need to talk further, at the rancho," he said. "So for now ... perhaps you will content yourself by asking my daughter if she would like to dance."

HEART'S DESIRE

❀

When a grinning Roger and blushing Francisca had joined the dancers in the plaza, Tía Magdalena beckoned Josefina aside. "It's good to see you, my child," she said. "And what a surprise to see Doña Felícitas, sitting there in the sun!"

"At first, I wasn't able to help her at all," Josefina confessed. "I kept trying, though." She looked up at her godmother. "I used to worry about remembering all the plants and remedios you're teaching me. Now I know there's a great deal more to understand about being a curandera."

Tía Magdalena smiled at her. "But becoming a curandera is still your heart's desire?"

Josefina looked at her family and friends, laughing and dancing and celebrating. *Happy.* "Sí," Josefina said simply. She had many things yet to learn ... but she knew, deep inside, that she was on the right path.

LOOKING BACK

A PEEK INTO THE PAST

New Mexico hills glow golden as the sun begins to set.

Tales of treasure have been part of New Mexican history for centuries. Rumors of seven fabulous cities built of gold first drew Spanish explorers to this remote territory nearly 500 years ago.

Such cities were never found, but as Spanish and Mexican colonists settled in New Mexico, new tales of treasure soon arose. New Mexican children today may still hear stories much like the ones Josefina heard at the harvest fiesta, and hopeful treasure seekers

A Spanish explorer

still venture into New Mexico's rugged hills.

Some legends tell of lost mines that hold rich veins of gold or silver. Others, like the story passed down in Pedro Zamora's family, tell of buried treasure, symbols carved into rock, and treasure maps. Some of the legends may actually be true. In the 1930s, a bar of gold and the grave of a Spanish soldier were found on top of a mesa that had been marked with faint carvings. In the 1950s, two matching halves of an old Spanish treasure map were found in northern New Mexico.

Many treasure stories are linked to the time of the Pueblo Revolt. In 1680, Pueblo Indians rose up after years of oppression and attacked Spanish forts and villages. Hundreds of colonists were killed, and the rest left New Mexico and fled south.

This map, drawn by a priest in 1826, stayed in New Mexico, but some of his maps ended up far away in Mexico.

In their haste to leave, people buried precious objects from their homes and churches, hoping to keep the treasures safe until the settlers could return. A map to one such treasure was later discovered under the altar of a burned church.

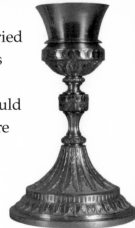

Religious objects, like this chalice, were often made of gold or silver.

Twelve years after the Pueblo Revolt, many settlers came back to New Mexico. No one knows if some of them retrieved their buried treasures then. But it is certain that life on the New Mexican frontier continued to hold many dangers—including the constant threat of attack and captivity. The Spanish and the Pueblo soon became allies and trading partners. But other Indians, such as the Navajo, Apache, and Comanche,

Spanish colonists fled from New Mexico during the bloody Pueblo Revolt.

raided Spanish settlements and Pueblo villages for livestock and food. Sometimes they burned homes and killed settlers. The Spanish raided their enemies just as fiercely.

Both sides took women and children as captives. Indians sometimes kept captives to do camp work or herd sheep—or even to become part of the family. But over the years, thousands of Indian and Spanish captives were sold as servants. Well-to-do New Mexican fathers often gave their daughters a *cautiva* as a wedding gift. In many towns, captives were sold in the main square.

Torn from their families and their culture, captives must have suffered greatly. Some escaped and made their way back home—although often their experiences as captives had changed them so much that home felt foreign, too. Most captives, like the Montoyas' servant Teresita,

Children as young as these Comanche girls were taken from many tribes.

did not escape and eventually adjusted to their new lives, but they probably never forgot the home they had left behind.

When Josefina was a girl in the 1820s, a new group of people began trickling into New Mexico as well—American traders from the United States. Like Roger Rexford, they were men who came on the Santa Fe Trail, crossing the plains between Missouri and New Mexico with wagon trains full of trade goods.

As a girl, this New Mexican woman was captured by Indians. Six years later, she escaped.

American traders unloading their wagons in Santa Fe

Although the English-speaking strangers seemed very foreign at first, the new trading opportunities they brought were welcome. Some New Mexicans—especially merchants and traders like Josefina's *abuelito*—developed strong business ties and friendships with Americans. Not surprisingly, *americanos* who decided to settle down in New Mexico often married girls from these traders' families.

Josefa Jaramillo, daughter of a New Mexican merchant, married Kit Carson, a scout who came west on the Santa Fe Trail. They enjoyed a long and happy marriage.